Surviving November

Stone Knight's MC
Book 7

Megan Fall

Surviving November
Published by Megan Fall

Dedication

To my readers

Without you I wouldn't be where I am today!

Contents

Surviving November

Chapter One – Jude

Chapter Two – May

Chapter Three – Jude

Chapter Four – May

Chapter Five – Jude

Chapter Six – May

Chapter Seven – Jude

Chapter Eight – May

Chapter Nine – Jude

Chapter Ten – May

Chapter Eleven – May

Chapter Twelve – May

Chapter Thirteen – Jude

Chapter Fourteen – May

Chapter Fifteen – Jude

Chapter Sixteen – Jude

Chapter Seventeen – May

Chapter Eighteen – Jude

Chapter Nineteen – Jude

Chapter Twenty – May

Chapter Twenty One – Jude

Chapter Twenty Two – May

Chapter Twenty Three – Jude

Chapter Twenty Four – May

Chapter Twenty Five – Jude

Chapter Twenty Six – May

Chapter Twenty Seven – Jude

Chapter Twenty Eight – May
Chapter Twenty Nine – Jude
Chapter Thirty – November
Chapter Thirty One – Jude
Chapter Thirty Two – Jude
Chapter Thirty Three – November
Chapter Thirty Four – Jude
Chapter Thirty Five – November
Chapter Thirty Six – Jude
Chapter Thirty Seven – November
Chapter Thirty Eight – Jude
Chapter Thirty Nine – November
Chapter Forty – Jude
Chapter Forty One – November
Chapter Forty Two – Jude
Chapter Forty Three – November
Chapter Forty Four – November
Chapter Forty Five – Jude
Chapter Forty Six – November
Chapter Forty Seven – Jude
Chapter Forty Eight – Jude
Chapter Forty Nine – November
Chapter Fifty – Jude
Chapter Fifty One – November
Chapter Fifty Two – Jude
Epilogue

Chapter 1
Jude

Jude stared at the moving truck as it pulled into the driveway next door. He had heard that someone had bought the house, but it had been vacant so long, he had given up hope that anybody would want it. It was a pretty little house, but it needed a ton of work. He pitied the person that had taken on a project that large. It would take a lot of time and money to complete the work it needed done.

When the truck stopped, two large guys stepped out and moved to the back, pulling up the rolling door.

Jude watched for hours, as piece after piece of flowery furniture was carried into the small house. Fascinated, he couldn't wait to see what crazy person was moving in.

In a couple hours they were done, and they pulled the rolling door down. As he watched, the men climbed back in the truck and were driving away. Jude had washed his Harley and cut the grass, in the time it had taken to empty the truck. When no one else came or went, he gave up watching. Climbing on his bike, he headed out to run the few errands he needed to do.

The grocery store was first. Jude ate out tons, so he pretty much only needed snacks. Even he'd admit he was a good cook, but with only him to cook for, he rarely bothered. His next stop was to the beer store, he was usually on his Harley, so it was impossible to cart the cases home. What he did instead was pay one of the stock boys to deliver it after his shift, it worked out well for both of them. The kid made a couple bucks, and Jude didn't have to take his truck to cart the beer home.

An hour later he was back. He unpacked the small amount of groceries he had bought, then headed outside, when he heard the roar of a motorcycle. Glancing up, he saw Navaho headed his way. The biker pulled in his driveway, shut down his Harley, and climbed off.

Navaho was a member of The Stone Knight's, the local biker club. They were all decent men, and Jude hung out with them often. They were bugging him to prospect, but Jude wasn't sure he would fit in. Most of the guys were honest, hard-working men, some were even military men, but Jude had done prison time. He didn't want to bring that kind of bad to a club that was respected.

Jude greeted Navaho with a grin and a half hug. The man didn't talk much, but he was good company. Navaho took a seat on one of the two chairs on the porch, while Jude went in for a six pack. Once it was on the porch between them and they each had a cold one, they got comfortable and shot the shit.

A couple hours later a sleek black car pulled up to the curb in front of the house next door. An old blue clunker, that sounded like it would backfire and take out the block, pulled into the drive. A big man in a suit got out of the fancy black car, while a tiny pixie, with long dark hair and glasses, got out of the clunker. She had her hands on her hips and her head tilted to the side, as she studied the small house.

"Hmm," Navaho mumbled. "Someone finally had the guts to buy that shit hole?" he asked, as he watched the scene unfolding in front of him. Jude knew they couldn't be seen as huge evergreen shrubs surrounded his porch.

"Guess so," Jude replied with a shrug. "Moving truck came today, flowery shit went in, then the moving truck left. If that idiots moving in with her, he's either gay, or he's whipped," he chuckled. Navaho snickered beside him.

The couple chatted for a minute, then the man hugged the pixie, kissed her on the head, then ruffled her dark curls. She fumed as she tried to swat him, but missed and fell flat on her ass. The man sighed, then helped her up and attempted to dust her off. That didn't go over so well, as they watched her kick him in the shin. Navaho chuckled again beside him.

"Guess they're not a couple," Navaho commented.

The man headed for his car, and the woman turned and headed for the steps. She tripped on the first one, but caught herself on the railing before she fell again. The man was already turning to head back, but she waved him off.

"Christ she's a klutz," Jude groaned, and Navaho nodded in agreement.

"You're going to have to keep on eye on that one. She's likely to burn down the house and take out yours with it," Navaho told him seriously.

"Fuck off," Jude huffed in annoyance. Then they watched as the man drove off, and the woman disappeared into the house.

Little did Jude know, that tiny pixie was about to become a huge pain in the ass.

Chapter 2
May

May stared at the boxes that surrounded her. She hated unpacking, and the thought of all she had to do was daunting. The guys had dumped the furniture wherever it fell, and the positioning was horrible. She'd have to climb over the chesterfield just to reach the kitchen. She bet they did that on purpose, just to see what she'd do. At five foot two, and a hundred and ten pounds, it would take everything she had to push it out of the way.

May eyed the rest of the room curiously. The coffee table was in front of the bathroom, and the armchair was pushed up against the closet. She sighed in agitation, hating how the boys loved to mess with her. She knew she'd have to figure out a way to get them back, it would be awhile before she saw any of them again, but she'd figure something out.

The guys that moved her, along with Colin, who had dropped her off, were all good friends with her brother. The men all worked together and acted more like siblings than coworkers. They had each other's backs, and they had hers too. The problem was, they all thought of her as their little sister. They teased her, they messed up her hair, and they chased away her dates. She loved them and equally hated them at the same time.

May headed to the bedroom, to see how messed up that was. Surprisingly, the bed was against the far wall, and her lounge chair was pushed into the corner. It was exactly the way she would have arranged it. She sighed in relief, pleased that she wouldn't have any work to do in here, except for some painting. The house was in extreme disrepair. Paint was peeling, and she could hear taps dripping from somewhere down the hall. She knew she'd have to investigate that soon, or else she feared she'd be waking up floating in bed.

May headed back into the living room, and dragged the boxes with her clothes down the hall, and into the bedroom. That was the bulk of the boxes, thank god. She had only brought the essentials with her, and the men had teased her relentlessly about what she considered essential. Her cloths were essential, her music was essential, and of course her pastels were essential.

As long as she could remember, she had been drawing. She carried a pack of pastels with her everywhere, and her clothing was usually covered with a variety of colours. Pastels were messy, and she loved it. Her pictures were abstract. She focused on the colours and swirled them into creative shapes. She loved her art work, and would be lost without it.

It didn't take May long to stuff her things in the dresser and closet, and then she sighed as she headed back out into the living room to face the heavy furniture once more. It was growing darker, so she turned on the lights, and stared out the huge windows.

With no curtains, people could see in, just as easily as she could see out. The front of the living room faced the street, and she loved how quiet it was. The other window faced directly into the house next door. The curtains in that house were open, but she was happy to see that no lights were on. At least no one would be watching her move things around.

May started with the coffee table, seeing as it was the smallest piece, and easily pushed it into the middle of the room. The armchair was harder, and it took muscling to get it where she wanted it. She eyed the chesterfield, and knew that no matter how she did this, it would be hard.

She moved to the end and pushed. It moved about two inches. Huffing, she turned around and backed into it. Then she pushed back with everything she had, using her feet for traction. It took her twenty minutes to get it under the window where she wanted it.

May brushed the hair out of her face with her hand and flopped down on the end. She was sweaty and sticky and knew she'd have to take a shower before bed. She glanced up and noticed the lights were now on in the house next door. And sitting in the window with a bottle of beer, was the biggest, most handsome, tattooed man she had ever seen.

It definitely looked like he had been watching her for a while. May was instantly pissed that he had watched her struggle, and hadn't come over to help. She stuck her tongue out at him, then smiled inwardly at the shock on his face. Standing, she turned to head towards her room, when she promptly tripped over the rug that was still rolled up on the floor.

Crying out, May fell, luckily only hitting her forehead. She cringed at the bruise she knew she'd be sporting tomorrow. Instead of standing, she crawled to her room, not wanting to face the laughter she could hear coming from the handsome assholes house. She cursed her new neighbour the entire way, and all the way through her cold shower. Another thing she'd have to fix.

May decided the first thing she would do, when she woke up the next day, was buy a set of curtains. The handsome asshole could find his amusement somewhere else.

Chapter 3
Jude

Jude had spent a long day at work, and he was tired and hungry. He had a job at the garage in The Stone Knight's compound. He loved working with the bikers, and got along with them all well, but he hated working on the shit cars that came in. His passion was muscle cars, but no garages in town specialized in them.

Jude was passing the hardware store, when he decided to pull in. He had broke the nozzle on his hose, and it would only take a minute to stop and buy a new one. He parked his Harley near the front door, shut it down, and climbed off. As soon as he turned to head to the door, he froze. Parked right beside him was the shit box the little klutz from next door drove. He wondered if it wouldn't be better to climb back on his bike and take off.

Sighing, and just wanting to get the damn nozzle and get out, Jude pushed open the door and headed inside. Keeping his head down, he headed straight to the garden section. When he turned the corner he was hit right in the midsection by a cart. He huffed as it knocked the wind out of him.

"Oh my god," a female voice shrieked from beside him. "I'm so sorry. I didn't see you, and you came around the corner so fast, you should really look before you do that, you could get hurt that way."

The girl would have continued, but Jude put up his hand, and she instantly quieted.

"Do you always talk this much?" he questioned as he raised his head to look at her. And of course, the girl standing in front of him now was the little klutz from next door.

Jude heard her suck in a breath as she looked up at him. She only came to his mid chest, so she had to lean way back to do it.

"Jesus, you're tall," she announced, as her nose scrunched up.

"And you're really short," Jude returned in annoyance.

She blinked, then glared at him. "You're the jerk from next door," she angrily accused. "You know you could have helped me move the furniture, instead of watching."

"But it was more entertaining my way," Jude smirked.

"I'm May," she informed him. "It's nice to meet you Lucy." Then she turned back to her cart, dismissing him.

He stood there in confusion for a minute before he slowly followed. "Why the fuck are you calling me Lucy, my names Jude?" he questioned.

She turned back to him for a minute and grinned big. "I don't like Jude", she declared, as she tilted her head to study him. "Lucy suits you better. I decided last night to call you Lucifer, but then I shortened it. Lucy's more fun." Then he had to jump out of the way, as the minx pushed past him with the cart, and ran over his foot.

"God damn it," Jude cursed, as he slammed into the rack behind him. He was fucking lucky he still had his steel-toed boots on from work. He glared at the girls back as she turned the corner. "And don't fucking call me Lucy," he growled loudly.

But of course she ignored him as she disappeared down the next isle. Jude shook his head, stomped to the garden section, grabbed his nozzle, and left the store as quickly as possible. The girl was in there somewhere, and he wanted out of the parking lot before she started driving.

Jude stopped at a burger joint on the way home and grabbed something to go. Minutes later he pulled into his driveway and shut off his Harley. He grabbed the nozzle and food from his saddlebag and headed inside. He was starving, so it only took him a minute to grab a beer, and wolf down his burger.

Jude turned to look at the nozzle and sighed, deciding to replace it before his shower. He swiped it off the counter and headed outside. Of course May was pulling into the driveway at the same time. She stopped, and the car made a big banging noise as it backfired. He watched as she got out, slammed the door, then kicked it when it wouldn't shut tight.

Jude chuckled as he headed to the side of his house where the hose was. In seconds he had the broken nozzle off, and the new one on. He headed back to the front of the house just in time to see her trip on a broken porch step. She dropped the bags and the cans of paint she was carrying, and they rolled down the walk.

Trying to be helpful, he gave her some much needed advice. "You may want to get that board replaced." She instantly whipped her head around to face him and glared.

"Fuck off Lucy," she yelled back angrily.

Then she stood, moved down the walk and retrieved her paint, then stomped into the house. Jude could only stare at her in shock, then he shook himself to clear his head and yelled back.

"Don't fucking call me Lucy," he shouted.

Then he too turned and stomped angrily into his house. He hated her, he really did hate her, he repeated to himself over and over.

Chapter 4
May

May finally had all her purchases from the hardware store picked up and stored in the corner of the living room. Even though she was only staying in this house for a short time, she needed to add colour to the walls. They were a dirty beige colour, and her artist's eye just couldn't take it. She figured she could paint the living room a bright yellow, then do a huge pastel canvas for the wall. It would make the house feel more like home.

May really missed her real home and her brother. They had always lived together and were closer than most brothers and sisters. She looked around the house sadly, she was lonely here, and the house was too quiet. She was used to her brother's friends barging in at all hours and bugging her. They treated her like a little sister, and she hated it. Sometimes she wanted them to see her as more.

Colin had been the one to drop her off, and she missed him the most. She had always had a small crush on him, but after years of him treating her like more of a sibling, she had gradually lost it. But she missed the noise her house always had.

That was something May could fix though, as the boys had been nice enough to set up her stereo in the room's corner. She hurried over and turned it on, hooking up her iPod to it. In minutes Chester Bennington's voice filled the room as Linkin Park's Burn It Down played. May smiled happily and ran into her room to put on a pair of cut-off shorts and a white tank.

When she came back into the living room she rolled out plastic, then poured some paint into a tray, and got down to work. May had bought a small roller to make the job easier, along with a step ladder. First though, she painted the corners and around the trim with a brush. This way, once she started rolling she could keep at it, as all the spots the roller couldn't get would be done.

May was about half way done when the smell of the paint started to get to her. She was on the step ladder, and the tray was on the top. She carefully set the brush in the tray and climbed down. Heading straight for the window in the living room, she pushed it open. Then she did the same with the front and back doors. She opened the storm doors so only the screen door was closed and lifted the screens in each door. Immediately, a gentle breeze blew through the house.

May sighed in relief as she headed to the stereo. The music was good, but Linkin Park was better turned up. She cranked the dial and grinned as the music went louder. Content, she climbed up the latter and got back to work. She sang as she painted to the beat of the song. She slapped the paint on the walls a bit faster and giggled when it splattered her. She knew it would be in her hair, on her clothes, and on her skin.

Laughing, and not caring at all, May continued on. She swayed a bit on the ladder as she moved to the beat of the music. This was the first time in weeks she could enjoy herself. She was completely immersed in what she was doing, so when she felt hands on her hips, she screamed and dropped the paint brush. Of course, the paint brush hit the paint tray and knocked it off the ladder.

"Jesus fucking Christ," May heard roared from below her. The hands on her hips gripped her tighter, and she was lifted off the ladder and placed on the floor.

May closed her eyes and stared at the floor, knowing immediately from the voice it was the handsome asshole. She raised her head and opened one eye to peek up at him. He was glaring down at her angrily, as yellow paint covered him from head to toe, and dripped onto the floor.

May couldn't help it, she bent over at the waist and laughed. She laughed so hard, she slipped on the paint and fell. As she lay on the floor, she kept laughing, not caring in the least she was laying in paint and Lucy was glaring down at her.

Chapter 5
Jude

Jude had been half asleep on the couch when the loud music woke him. He twisted and placed his feet on the floor, then hefted himself up. Growling, he stomped over to the window and peered out. Sure enough, the pretty little klutz had all the windows open, and it was her house the music was coming from.

He headed out his front door and prowled across the lawn to climb up her porch steps. Carefully, he stepped over the broken one as he headed for the front door. When he couldn't find a doorbell, he gave up, and pounded on the side of the screen door.

He was concerned when the poor door rattled and looked like it was about to come down.

Jude stood there a minute, waiting for her to answer, but she never did. Sighing, he gently pulled the door open and stepped inside. He was even more pissed to see the screen wasn't locked, anyone could have walked in on her and she'd never know. He looked around the room, searching for her, then stood there in stunned silence.

The little klutz was standing on a ladder, painting the walls. She had on a tiny pair of shorts, a tight white tank, and her feet were bare. She was obviously enjoying herself, as she sang and swayed to the music. He couldn't take his eyes off her, she was absolutely breathtaking.

The swaying had caught his attention. The girl had no idea that the ladder was tipping each time she moved. Furious once more, he stomped over to her and placed his hands on her hips to hold her still. He could do nothing but stare at her in dread, as she screamed and dropped the brush. It hit the paint tray and knocked it over.

Knowing what would happen, but not being able to do a god damned thing about it, he closed his eyes and waited. He wasn't disappointed, as yellow paint hit him in the head and covered him from head to

toe. Then, the paint tray bounced off as well and fell
to the floor. Beyond mad now, he lifted her off the
ladder, and stood her on the floor in front of him.

When Jude opened his eyes and looked down at her,
it was to find hers squeezed shut tightly. He smirked
as she opened one and peeked up at him. He bit his
lip to hold in the chuckle at the sight of her
expression. She looked almost terrified for a minute,
then it changed to one of laughter. That was when
she lost her balance and fell on the floor. After a
minute he placed his hands on his hips and glared at
her once more.

"Are you almost done?" Jude growled. May looked
up at him, blinked, and started laughing again.

Deciding he'd had enough, Jude leaned over and
picked her up, causing her to squeal. The girl had
almost as much paint on her as he did, and she didn't
get it over her head.

"Why are you in my house?" May questioned,
causing him to glare down at her.

"Because I was sleeping, and your god damned
music woke me up," Jude told her.

"Well why didn't you knock on the door?" she
questioned.

Jude couldn't stop the growl that rumbled from deep in his chest. "I did, but the god damned thing almost fell off when I hit it."

May squinted at him as she studied his arms. "Well maybe you should try using a little less muscle," she replied helpfully.

Jude conveniently ignored her as he headed to her stereo and turned it down. When he turned back to face her, she looked incredibly sad as she stared down at the stereo.

"It was too quiet," May whispered, and he could tell she didn't mean for him to hear her.

He frowned at her as he saw a small tear slip down her cheek. But before he could question her, she turned away and started to clean up the mess on the floor.

"You better wash that paint off while you can," May told him. He knew a dismissal when he heard one, so he turned and headed for the door.

"Lock your door behind me," he demanded, in as soft a voice as he could manage. Then he headed out and crossed the lawn, but the sight of that lone tear bothered him. The klutzy little neighbour was getting to him, and he didn't know if he was ready for that.

Chapter 6
May

May stayed up late into the night and finished painting the living room. She had kept the music on, but left it at the volume Lucy had put it at. She certainly didn't want him stomping over again and getting in her face. Luckily, the paint that had gotten on the floor washed off easily. Not that it mattered, the wood floors were a disaster. They were scuffed, they had stains on them, and they were a faded out colour. But she knew she wouldn't be here long enough to make it worthwhile to refinish them.

Sighing, she cleaned up her paint cans, rolled up the drop cloths, and cleaned the brush and roller. The paint colour did make the room look cheerier, so that boosted her spirits somewhat. She pushed the furniture back, but made sure it didn't touch the still-wet walls.

Collapsing into a chair by the window, May stared at the dark house next door. The handsome ass had gone to bed earlier, and for that she was grateful. She had bought curtains, but had decided to paint before putting them up. Tomorrow she would do that first thing.

When her eyes started to close, May knew it was time for bed. She pushed out of the chair and headed for the bathroom. She knew she needed a quick shower first. When she closed the door and looked in the mirror, she couldn't help but laugh. There was paint on her nose, paint on her cheek, paint in her eyes brows, and of course paint in her dark hair. She really hoped the shampoo got it out, because any other chemical would most likely take the dark dye out too. If it didn't come out, she'd have to live with yellow hair for a while.

May undressed, turned on the water, and laid a towel out. After a minute, the water was finally warm enough to step into. She relaxed and let it sooth her sore arms and aching neck. Painting had worked muscles she didn't even know she had. She dumped shampoo on her palm and lathered up her hair, then rinsed it and did it again. Next came the conditioner, her long hair was a knotted mess if she didn't use it.

May turned to the soap and was about to wash the rest of her body when the water turned icy cold. Screaming for all she was worth, she tried to jump out from under the spray. Of course the conditioner had made the tub slippery, and she quickly lost her balance. Still screaming, May gripped the shower curtain, but instead of it stopping her fall, it broke from the rod and went down with her. She cried out, as her head slammed against the side of the toilet.

Dazed, May lay there for a minute trying to figure out how that happened. When she glanced up at the shower, it was to see the cold water still shooting out of the shower head. Without the shower curtain up, it was now hitting the floor, and she was still getting wet.

Cursing, May attempted to untangle herself from the curtain, when the door suddenly crashed in and she found herself staring at the handsome ass once more. Knowing she was completely naked and probably putting on quite a show, she tried to reach for the towel, but the damned shower curtain only got tangled more. She had no choice but to give up, and stay where she was, staring at Lucy wearily.

"What the ever loving fuck," Lucy roared in anger. "I thought someone was killing you."

"Not yet," May mumbled, as she pushed the wet hair out of her face. "Did you break down my door with those freaking muscles of yours?" she questioned, as she blinked up at him in an attempt to keep the cold water out of her eyes.

Jude growled, then she watched happily as he climbed over her to shut off the water. "Fuck that's cold," he complained.

May tilted her head and frowned up at him. "No shit Sherlock," she replied in annoyance. "Now can you please fuck off, so I can get myself out of this mess," she ordered.

Jude looked down at her and smiled. "But I'm enjoying the view," he teased.

She closed her eyes in exasperation, then quickly opened them again when he bellowed at her.

"You're fucking bleeding."

Uh oh, was all she could think before he was heading for her and crouching down.

Chapter 7
Jude

Jude stared at the pretty little klutz lying naked on the floor. Unfortunately, the plastic shower curtain covered most of her body, but the sight of her still took his breath away. She was fucking beautiful. He almost chuckled as she tried to get up, but was hampered by the curtain. Somehow he didn't think she'd appreciate his laughter right now.

Then his attention turned to a spot on her forehead, where blood was slowly dripping. "You're fucking bleeding," he roared, as he crouched down and moved towards her.

May shrieked and tried to cover herself, as she held up her hand to stop him. "Don't you dare come any closer," she ordered.

But he just scowled at her and knocked her hand out of the way. When he got close, he swiped the towel off the counter and covered her, shower curtain and all. Then he grabbed a washcloth and leaned over her so he could get a better look. The first thing he noticed was how she shivered as she stared up at him.

"You afraid of me little klutz?" Jude questioned gently, as he brushed the hair away from the cut.

Her back straightened, and she looked away from him. "No," she stammered. "I'm cold. A soak in some icy water will do that."

Jude smirked at her. "Right," he stated. When he leaned closer, he realized the cut was pretty deep. He placed the washcloth against it as gently as he could, but she still cried out.

"Sorry," he apologized. "The first thing we need to do is get you off this god damned floor," he told her. "You hold on to that towel while I stand you up," he instructed. Then he placed his hands under her arms and hefted her up. She squealed, as she tried to hold on to the towel. As soon as she was on her feet, the curtain dropped to the ground.

"Thank you," May sighed as she took a deep breath to calm herself. Then he watched in disappointment as she pulled the towel tighter against her.

"You need stitches," Jude growled.

May shook her head stubbornly. "I'll be fine," she quietly decided. "Iodine and a bandage and I'll be good as new. Now thank you for your help, but I need you to leave so I can get dressed."

Jude smirked at her, as he looked down at the skin not covered by the towel. "Please don't get dressed on my account," he teased her. "I think you should wear a towel all the time."

She glared at him as she shoved him roughly out the bathroom door. Once he was on the other side, the lock clicked. He chuckled at the closed door, but she must have heard him.

"Fuck off Lucy," was yelled from inside. He instantly stopped laughing and growled at the door in frustration. Turning, he made his way to the living room and sat on the couch. He pulled out his cell and scrolled through his contacts until he found the name he was looking for. Then he hit a button to connect the call.

"Sniper," Jude greeted after the man answered. "I know it's late, but would Doc be up?" he asked.

"He sure is, you okay?" the biker questioned in return.

"It's not for me," Jude explained. "My neighbour fell and hit her forehead pretty good. The cuts deep, and she needs a couple stitches."

Sniper chuckled. "Oh, you mean the klutz. Navaho told us about the two of you watching her move in."

Jude hung his head. "That's the one," he admitted.

"Kind of late to be over there," the noisy fucker pushed.

"She screamed when she fell, and I heard her. Broke the door down and found her bleeding on the floor," Jude admitted.

Sniper's voice instantly changed. "Right, me and Raid will come too. We'll get the door fixed," he promised.

"Appreciated," Jude replied as he hung up. Now all he had to do was wait for May to come out of the bathroom and then deal with the fallout when the three big bikers showed at her door.

Chapter 8
May

May got dressed in some sweats and one of her brothers old tee shirts. Then she brushed her hair and threw some spare towels down to sop up the water. Her head was a mess, but there wasn't much she could do about it because she couldn't go to the hospital. She got out a clean washcloth and held it on the cut. She knew that unless she got the bleeding to slow down, the bandage wouldn't stick.

Sighing, when it didn't look like it was working, May opened the door and headed into the living room. She froze as soon as she noticed the handsome ass sitting on the couch.

"Oh, come on," May complained tiredly. "I asked you to leave. Why can't you just listen?"

"Because you have a head injury, and you won't go to the hospital," Jude replied as he glanced over at her.

May ignored him as she got a good look at her front door. The screen looked fine, but the door itself was cracked around the handle, and she could see the bottom hinge was the only thing keeping it from falling off.

"Did you run through it?" she questioned in shock.

"No smart ass," Jude chuckled. "I kicked it with my boot. The doors old as fuck, it should have been a lot harder to get in," he said with a frown.

May turned to look out the front window, when the roar of motorcycles sounded from the street. As she watched, they pulled into her driveway and parked near the house. She backed away from the window fearfully, as she eyed the two big men heading for her door. She barely saw the SUV that pulled in behind them.

"Those are friends of mine," Jude announced, as he stood and headed for the door.

"Then why aren't they going to your house?" she inquired.

"Because I called them, and asked them to come here," Jude patiently explained as he opened the door for them. She stared at them as they prowled inside and stopped to look at her.

"Wow the klutz is pretty," one of them said. She blinked as she continued to stare at him. Then she turned to Jude and shook her finger at him.

"Stop telling people I'm a klutz," May ordered.

The handsome ass shrugged. "Stop doing stupid shit that gets you hurt," he argued back.

"I don't do it on purpose," May yelled, as she threw up her arms in frustration.

"Oh," Jude snickered. "So trouble just finds you?" he countered.

May caught the two bikers looking back and forth between each of them while they argued.

"Oh this will be fun," one of them smirked.

She turned to him in annoyance, when a third man walked through the door, carrying a medical bag.

"Hello sweetheart," he greeted, as he headed straight for her. "Names Doc. These two bikers are Raid and Sniper. They told me that you have a head wound that needs some attention," he stated kindly.

May nodded at him as she looked back over to Jude. "And why are they here?" she asked, pointing at the bikers.

"To fix the door I ran through," Jude smirked.

"Right," May responded, as if it was a normal occurrence.

"What's your name darling?" Doc asked.

She went to answer and then stopped herself. Blinking, she looked at him, then replied "May".

"Are you sure?" Doc chuckled.

She looked down at the floor. "I'm sure," she whispered.

"Okay then," Doc replied. "How about if you have a seat on the couch, and I'll see about fixing you up?" She nodded and headed to the couch. When she sat, she saw the two bikers head over to the door and check it out.

Doc opened his bag and pulled things out, then told her to take the cloth off her head. She jumped in surprise when Jude sat down beside her.

"This may hurt," Doc warned as he prodded at the wound. "Definitely needs four stitches," he told her after a minute. "I'll give you a quick shot to numb the area, then I'll get to work. It won't take long."

"Okay," May replied somewhat quietly, then whimpered when the needle went in. She was thankful when Jude wrapped his arm around her shoulders, and left it there as Doc stitched her up.

Chapter 9
Jude

Jude shocked himself, when he unconsciously sat beside May and held her, as Doc stitched her up. She was a pretty little klutz, but she was a pain in his ass. His only excuse was that he hated to see her in pain. It had really bothered him when he first saw the blood.

Once Doc was done, and her wound was covered, he let her go. He watched as Doc gave her some pain meds and told her not to get it wet for a couple days. She thanked him, then Doc gathered up his things, making her promise to call if she needed him again, and left.

When Jude looked over at Raid and Sniper, he was happy to see the bikers had the door back in place and reattached.

"It's a temporary fix," Sniper explained. "It will do for now, but she needs a new door."

"I'll see to it," Jude promised. Then he shook hands with them both as they cleaned up their mess.

"You coming on the ride tomorrow?" Sniper questioned. Several members of the club were heading out for a ride in the morning, then checking out a new diner a couple towns over. They frequently invited Jude, and he rarely said no. He nodded at the brother in acceptance.

"You want to ride to the club and meet us, or you want us to pick you up on the way?" Raid asked.

"Swing by and grab me," Jude replied with a smirk.

The bikers chuckled. "Gotcha," Sniper agreed, then they turned and left.

Jude shut the door and headed back to the couch, where his pretty little klutz was still sitting.

"I never asked what you hit your head on?" he questioned curiously.

May eyed him a minute before answering. "None of your business," she finally told him.

"Ah," he chuckled. "So it was the toilet."

She glared at him. "Why do you think that?"

"Because if it was anything else you would have told me," Jude smirked knowingly.

"You're such an ass," May told him for the hundredth time.

Jude chuckled, then stared at her shirt. It was a guys shirt, he could tell right away. It looked like an old baseball shirt, one a boyfriend would give a girlfriend to wear.

"Nice shirt," he huffed.

"Thanks," she answered, but offered nothing else.

"An old boyfriends?" Jude pushed with a raised brow.

May looked at him in surprise. "No, it's my brother's," she told him. "I stole it when he grew out of it. I like it because it's well worn and soft," she admitted.

"Your brother and you are close?" Jude inquired, happy to finally get some personal information from her.

May immediately smiled, and it lit up her face. "The closest," she told him.

"When do I get to meet him?" Jude asked curiously.

As he watched the smile instantly slipped from her face. "I'm exhausted," she suddenly announced. "It's late and my head hurts. I think it's time for you to go, I need to head to bed." She stood then and walked over to the door, opening it and waiting for him.

Jude knew a brushoff when he heard one, and she was definitely avoiding answering his question. With the head wound though, he let her have her way and not push it.

"Okay," he replied, as he rose to his feet and headed out the door. "But I'm right next door. If your head bothers you too much, just scream and I'll come running," he smirked in an attempt to lighten the mood.

He was happy to see a smile grace her face. "Thanks Lucy," she chuckled, as she shut and locked the door on him.

"Don't fucking call me that," he growled loudly as he walked away. A god damned pain in the ass he thought, as he made his way across the lawn. He went in his own house, shut and locked the door and headed to bed.

He really needed some sleep. The bikers were planning to leave at seven in the morning, so they could enjoy a long ride before hitting up the diner. He smirked as he thought about May. She woke him up with her music, so he wondered how she would like it when a dozen motorcycles roared down the street while she was trying to sleep. He soon drifted off, and he did it with a huge smile on his face.

Chapter 10
May

It didn't take May long to fall asleep. She was absolutely exhausted, but thankfully her head didn't hurt thanks to Doc's pills. It felt like she had only been asleep for a few minutes, when loud thunder woke her, and her poor little house shook. The thunder just kept getting louder and louder, and a brush fell off her nightstand.

May threw her legs over the side of the bed and stood. Groggily, she wandered through the house and noticed the sound was continuous. Thunder had a loud bang, and then it stopped for while before banging again, so maybe it wasn't thunder. She watched in fascination as the paint can opener she had used last night bounced across her coffee table. When it hit the floor, she blinked, and shook her head.

Finally, May turned to face the front window. Without curtains, she had a good view of the street. Her mouth dropped open when she saw at least a dozen motorcycles parked in front of her house. Still half asleep, she unlocked the front door, and stepped out onto the porch. She couldn't quite comprehend why they were out there, but all at once the bikers turned in her direction.

"Now there's a sight I'd like to wake up to every morning," one of the bikers yelled her way. A couple others actually whistled. May had just woken up, so she couldn't figure out why they were whistling at her.

"Come over here darling and hop on the back of my bike. I'll take you for a ride," the same biker that yelled out before beckoned.

"Fuck off Dagger," May heard roared from Jude's driveway. When she looked that way, she saw the handsome ass himself. He was climbing off his bike and heading right for her. Uh oh she thought, as she took in his furious expression.

Jude looked good for an angry man, and that pissed her off. He had on worn jeans with a hole in the knee, biker boots, a black tee and a worn black leather jacket. Black was her new favourite colour she immediately decided.

"What the fuck have you got on?" Jude roared as he marched across the lawn. Unsure of what he was so mad about, she looked down at her brothers shirt, then back at him.

"A tee shirt," she answered in confusion.

"What else?" he growled from the bottom of her porch.

May looked down again and realized what he meant. She only ever slept in the tee and panties. She always removed the sweats before climbing into bed.

"Well, you and your biker buddies woke me up from a dead sleep," May furiously told him. "Plus I hit my head and was given medicine not that long ago. Sorry if my state of dress offends you."

"Oh I like her, she's feisty," the one Jude had called Dagger yelled.

Then Sniper yelled out too. "I think your plan backfired." She remembered him from last night and waved. He chuckled and waved back.

"Fuck me," Jude cursed. "You're standing on the porch in a fucking tee and waving at a bunch of bikers."

"I was just being friendly," May argued back.

"Well it would be nice if you could be friendly while wearing fucking pants," he growled. Then she watched as he placed his boot on her broken porch step and fell right through it.

The bikers all laughed, and she cringed when Jude looked up at her like he was about to lose it. His face was pinched, his hands were fisted, and his teeth were clenched tight.

"You need to be careful on those steps, they're broken," May helpfully told him.

"Feisty and funny," Dagger yelled once more, adding fuel to the fire. "My dream woman."

May opened her mouth to shout something back, but then noticed Jude was trying to pull his foot out of the porch. She immediately understood that when he was free, she was in trouble. She backed up quickly until she was safely in the doorway.

"I'm still extremely exhausted," May announced. Then added a long, drawn out yawn for effect. "I think I'll head back to bed." Then she squealed when he got his foot out.

"Have a nice ride Lucy," she chuckled, as she slammed the front door shut and locked it.

"Don't fucking call me Lucy," she heard growled from the handsome ass.

"Come on Lucy," someone bellowed. "Get on your fucking bike, or we're leaving without you."

May heard Jude growl again as he stomped away. "My fucking name's Jude," he declared to a bunch of howling bikers.

Chapter 11
May

May was in a bad mood. Her head hurt and she was still unbelievably tired. After all the bikers left, she had a terrible time falling back to sleep. She lay there counting the cracks in the ceiling for about two hours, then gave up and dragged herself out of bed. She threw her hair in a messy bun and grabbed her glasses. She had been wearing them on and off since she got here, and she figured she needed to wear them more.

May headed to the kitchen and made herself a quick bowl of cereal, then plopped down lazily on the couch to eat it. Her thoughts moved to all the bikers she had seen earlier this morning. They were huge, muscled and handsome, but none of them held a candle to the handsome ass.

The problem was, May didn't know what to feel about that. Jude was extremely good looking, but he drove her up the wall. He only had to be in the room for a couple minutes before they'd argue. But when he had held her as Doc put the stitches in, it had felt right, and it had felt like something more.

She'd had a crush on Colin for so long it was hard to think of anyone else. But that crush died when he hadn't returned her affection. She thought about Jude for a minute. He was definitely better looking, and when he touched her, it felt incredibly amazing. Colin had given her many hugs over the years, but they hadn't come close to the way she felt when Jude touched her.

May shook her head and stood up. She had things to do, she didn't have time to dwell on that. The first thing she wanted to do was put up her curtains. She'd had enough of Jude watching her from his house. The curtains she bought were a pretty light blue plaid, and she knew they'd look cute with the yellow walls.

May hooked up her iPod to the stereo and got to work. There was already a curtain rod there, so that made things a lot easier. She opened the package and spread out the curtains across the couch. Then she grabbed her step ladder and dragged it over to the window. Carefully, she unhooked the rod from each side and brought it down. It only took her a minute to thread the curtains through and drag it back over to the window.

May slowly climbed back on the step stool with the curtains in hand and hooked on one end with no trouble. Grinning, she climbed back down in order to move the ladder to the other end. As soon as she got down the curtain on the side she was holding slid off. She huffed as she tried to hold the end and pick up the curtain off the floor. She stretched as far as she could, but she still couldn't reach while holding the rod. Frustrated now, she let go to grab the curtain on the floor. As soon as she did, the other curtain slid down the rod and slipped off, draping completely over her.

Cursing a blue streak, May tried to shove it off, when she heard the unmistakable sound of laughter. Immediately she froze. She knew that laughter, she'd certainly heard it enough over the last couple days to know who it belonged to.

"I thought you were on a motorcycle ride?" May huffed from under the curtain. She decided staying under the curtain was her best bet, so she sat on the floor and got comfortable.

"I was, but it was only a morning ride. We had an early lunch and headed back. Good timing if you ask me, I'm glad I didn't miss this," Jude chuckled.

"How long have you been watching?" she sighed, knowing she wouldn't like his answer.

"Since you opened the curtains. I had a good view from outside the window, but then you bent down and I lost sight of you. I had to hustle inside to catch the rest," he admitted.

"Of course you did," May growled in return. Then she screeched as the curtain was ripped away and she was knocked to her back. "You're an ass," she told him from her sprawled position on the floor.

"So you've repeatedly told me," Jude smirked. Then he surprised her by offering his hand. She eyed it warily for a minute too long, because he sighed. "I'm not going to hurt you."

"I know," May acknowledged. "I'm looking for the buzzer."

"The what?" he questioned in confusion.

"You know, the thing you hold in your hand so when someone takes it they get a shock," May explained with a serious expression.

"You're a goof," he laughed, as he took her hand and hauled her to her feet. He pulled a little too hard though, because her entire body crashed into his. When she found the courage to look up at him, he was staring down at her with a weird expression on his face.

Chapter 12
May

May stared up at Jude as they stood chest to chest. She had completely frozen when he pulled her up and she fell against him. Now she barely breathed as she stood there wondering what to do. He was incredibly warm, and the smell of him was intoxicating. She almost swayed closer towards him, but stopped herself in time.

Suddenly Jude leaned down towards her. She couldn't even blink, he had her undivided attention. He stopped when his lips were almost touching hers.

"Breathe," Jude whispered, causing her to shiver.

Finally May blinked, as she let out the huge breath she had no idea she'd been holding. As soon as she was done his lips softly touched hers. She relaxed completely and melted against him, as she felt his hand snake up under her hair and clamp onto the back of her neck. He deepened the kiss as soon as he felt her compliance, and she was lost to him. His breath and her breath became one. She wrapped her arms around him and held on as tight as she could.

After a minute Jude broke away and looked down at her in annoyance. She was dazed, so she didn't understand why. The only thing she could come up with was that maybe he didn't like it. She dropped her head in embarrassment and tried to pull away.

"I think your cell's ringing," Jude announced as he kept a tight hold on her.

"What?" May questioned in complete confusion. Jude chuckled at her, and it was then she heard the definite sound of her cell. She instantly pulled away and hurried towards the stereo.

"How long has it been ringing?" she asked as panic set in.

When she glanced back at Jude he looked agitated, and she knew he was picking up on her panic. She hurried to grab the cell, but dread filled her when it stopped ringing.

"Damn it," May cried, as she stopped the music and searched for the last number that called. Her finger was hovering over the button when it rang again. This time she got it on the first ring. She didn't even get a word in, when Colin started yelling.

"Why the fuck didn't you pick up?" he demanded, causing her to deflate and hang her head.

"I didn't hear it, I'm sorry," May apologized. "Then it stopped ringing when I reached it."

"You okay?" Colin questioned still visibly upset.

"I'm fine," she quietly told him. Then she jumped as Jude suddenly appeared beside her. He placed his large hand on her back and soothingly rubbed up and down.

"You were playing your music too loud again," Colin correctly guessed, and she couldn't help but smile.

"I like my music," May felt the need to add.

"I know squirt," Colin chuckled, and she could hear the smile in his voice.

"Don't call me that," May complained in annoyance "Why did you call anyway?"

"I wanted to let you know I have a day off tomorrow, so I'm coming for dinner," Colin announced. She missed all her brother's friends so much, the thought of seeing him excited her.

"You're coming for dinner?" May repeated happily. "Just you or everybody?" she squealed.

"Sorry squirt, you just get me," Colin told her with a chuckle.

"Is that a good idea?" she asked, trying to be careful of what she said in front of Jude.

"It will be okay," Colin promised. "I'll be careful." Then they said their goodbyes, and she hung up. She was so excited she was practically jumping up and down when she turned to face Jude.

"Who's coming to dinner?" he questioned curiously.

"Colin, he's a friend of mine," May happily told him. But his face darkened at her answer, putting a damper on her mood.

"A friend of yours?" Jude asked while scowling down at her. She took a tentative step back as she looked at him curiously, having no idea why he was so angry.

"A close friend?" he nearly growled, and it finally dawned on her what he was getting at. Angry now, she placed her hands on her hips and glared back at him.

"Yes," she returned. "But if you think after one kiss you can start that shit, you're wrong."

"Oh I don't think so," Jude told her as he closed the distance she had put between them. "I know so." Then he took one more step towards her, placing them chest to chest once more. "I'm coming to dinner," he demanded.

"No you're not," May quickly responded.

"Yes I am," he growled furiously. "That kiss was the best fucking kiss I've ever had, and I'm going to want to do that again. And you can bet after that I will not let you have dinner with another man unless I'm here."

"Oh," she replied as she blinked up at him in surprise. "You like me Lucy."

Jude growled again, took her lips once more in a searing kiss, then turned and walked out the door. May ran to the window and watched him stomp across the lawn. It was then she realized she had no idea how this would work.

Chapter 13
Jude

Jude had no idea what to expect as he got ready for dinner. As soon as they ended kiss his pretty little klutz had made dinner plans with another guy, and that pissed him off. He had been completely surprised by the way that kiss had affected him. It had literally knocked him off his feet. He had never felt that much chemistry or attraction before.

The men from The Stone Knight's had this ridiculous idea about finding The One. They claimed that when you found her, you knew she was meant to be with you. It's like you stop breathing for a minute the first time you meet her. Jude had repeatedly told the men it was a load of crap, but he had to admit, he definitely felt that way the first time he was close to May.

And what pissed him off was that he hadn't been ready for it. He was happy with his life the way it was, and he wasn't ready for any complications. And she was definitely a complication. The girl got in more trouble in one day than he had in years. If he was with her, he'd have to be on his toes twenty-four hours a day. But at the same time, life with her would never be boring.

Jude scowled, already in a bad mood, as he tied his boots and headed out the door. The little klutz better be careful tonight, because it had been a while since he had been in a good fight, and he was due.

He decided he wasn't going to knock as he headed for the porch. When he looked down and noticed the steps, he did a double take. The hole where his foot had gone through was still there, but May had painted the surrounding area the same yellow she had dumped on his head. Now there was no way he could miss it as he climbed up. He shook his head, deciding that would be the first thing he fixed tomorrow.

When Jude made it successfully to the top, he pushed the door open and strode right in. He glanced around the room, then went straight to the window with the curtains still not up. She had pushed the ladder to the side, the rod was still hanging from the one side that was actually attached, and the curtains were draped over a chair. He sighed knowing May must have given up, and moved the ladder back under the rod. In less than a minute he had slid on the curtains and hooked it back into place.

"Thank you," Jude heard his klutz say from close behind him. He climbed down, folded up the ladder, and placed it in the corner. "I just couldn't reach to finish it, and I didn't want to risk another injury," May explained.

When Jude turned to face her, he could only stare in absolute fascination. She was wearing a cute little dress with short sleeves. It had elastic under her breasts that made the dress flare out to just above her knees. Her hair was down, her glasses were on, and she wore a bit of makeup.

"You're fucking beautiful," Jude couldn't resist telling her. Then he sucked in a breath when she smiled at him in complete happiness. She looked like a god damned angel. "You should go change," he told her as his scowled returned. "Maybe put on a pair of jeans, and an old sweatshirt," he advised.

May blinked as she looked at him in confusion. "But you said I looked beautiful."

"I said you look fucking beautiful," Jude corrected. "But the prick coming tonight will see you looking like that too," he growled.

May was about to say something when the doorbell rang, interrupting him. She squealed and ran to answer it, and he scowled at the obvious excitement she was showing. He hurried after her and caught her before she got to it. Not bothering to explain himself, he grabbed her arm, spun her around, and pulled her into his arms. She looked so pretty staring up at him in surprise.

Then Jude's lips crashed against hers, and he was kissing her for all he was worth. She soon relaxed against him, threw her arms around his waist, and kissed him back just as enthusiastically. Encouraged, he placed his hand on the back of her head and deepened the kiss, causing her legs to give out. He easily took all her weight, then after a minute pulled back.

May's hair was messy, her face and chest were flushed, and her lips were swollen. But it was the dazed expression on her face that made him smile the most.

"Now you can answer the door," Jude smugly declared, after it had rung for the third time.

Chapter 14
May

May was still reeling from Jude's kiss when she opened the door. The man certainly knew what he was doing. Colin stood on the porch and stared at her for a minute, obviously studying her, before he engulfed her in a bear hug and spun around.

"Hey squirt," he greeted happily. "You look flushed. Your not getting sick are you?"

May instantly bristled. "Don't call me that," she ordered. But he only laughed at her as he kept spinning her.

"Squirt huh," she heard echoed from behind her.

With Colin still spinning her, all she could do was yell.

"Shut up Lucy," she hurled in Jude's direction.

"Don't call me that," Jude growled in return. Then Colin was grabbed by the arm, and thankfully the spinning stopped. It was killing her head and making her dizzy. Suddenly she was plucked out of Colin's arms, and she found herself hanging from Jude's instead. Gratefully, she laid her head on his shoulder. As soon as she did that he scooped up her legs and carried her inside, sitting down with her on his lap.

"Who the fuck are you?" Colin bellowed as he followed them inside and slammed the door shut. But Jude ignored him as he placed his warm hand on her chin and titled her face up to look at him.

"You okay?" Jude questioned softly. May looked up at him as the pounding in her head eased slightly.

"No, but it's getting better," she admitted. "I just need another minute." Then she brushed his hand away and put her head back against his chest. His chest shook, and she knew he was laughing at her.

"I think you need more medicine," Jude stated after giving her another minute.

"Why the fuck do you need medicine?" Colin roared, and as an afterthought added, "and get the fuck off him."

"She's got a head injury you ass," Jude growled in annoyance. "And she can stay where she is for as long as she likes," he taunted.

"I'm going to ask you one more time who you are, then I'm just going to shoot you," Colin snarled right back. May finally had enough, she pushed off Jude's lap, stuck her hands on her hips, and glared at the two.

"Are you both finished?" she asked with a bite to her words. "I'm hungry and my head hurts, and you're acting like jerks," she announced.

"I'm Jude," the handsome ass declared. "And you must be Colin."

"Yes, I'm Colin," Colin sneered. Then he turned to her. "I left you here a week ago. Suddenly you have a new friend and you've done something stupid to hurt your head. What the fucks going on?"

"I'm not her friend," Jude smugly interrupted. "I'm her man."

"What?" both May and Colin said at the same time. "No you're not," May added as an afterthought.

"The fuck I'm not," Jude growled as he stood to his full height and approached her. She raised her hand to stop him, but as usual he ignored it. The ass scooped her up and kissed her again, and she forgot all about what they were arguing about. When he finally let her go, she could only stare up at him.

"Now," Jude demanded, while he smiled down at her. "Are you mine?"

"Uh huh," May answered as she blinked up at him. Then she shook her head and slapped his arm.

"What the hell did you do that for?" Jude asked as he rubbed the spot.

"Because you did that on purpose," she told him.

"Well it's the easiest way to get you to stop arguing with me," he told her smugly. "And I like doing it," The ass added.

"I wasn't arguing with you," May yelled as she threw up her arms in agitation.

"You fucking were," Jude growled back. "You're doing it now," he replied as he too threw up his hands.

Frustrated, she turned away from him and faced Colin. But her friend had his head tilted and was staring at her differently.

"You've changed honey," Colin told her in a lower voice. "You've got a dress on, you've gotten a backbone, and you look really pretty."

May looked at him in confusion, floored by his declaration. "You think I look pretty?" she asked. Then she squealed when Jude wrapped his arm around her stomach and slammed her back into his chest.

"Don't you fucking dare," Jude accused as he glared at Colin murderously. "It seems you've known her for a long time, and you had your chance. Now she's mine, so you can fuck off and find your own woman," Jude snarled. "Or do I have to kiss her again to prove it."

May immediately titled her head up to look back at Jude. "I think you should kiss her again to prove it," she answered with a huge grin.

Chapter 15
Jude

Jude hated Colin before he even stepped foot in the
door. The fucker had an air of authority he didn't
like. Jude had so many previous run-ins with the
law, that he knew a cop when he saw one. And this
ass was definitely one. He decided he'd have to keep
a close eye on him.

"So what do you do for a living Colin?" Jude
questioned casually, as they were finally sitting down
to dinner. May was dishing out plates of spaghetti,
and there was a basket of warm bread in the middle
of the table. As soon as he asked though May's head
jerked up, and she turned to face Colin.

"I'm in banking," Colin smoothly answered.
"Investments and stocks. And what do you do?" he
fucker questioned in return.

Jude shrugged. "Little of this, little of that. Right now I work as a mechanic at The Stone Knight's compound."

Colin almost sneered at that answer. "You work on cars."

Jude hated when people looked down on him. "I fucking do. But I hope to open a garage of my own one day and restore old muscle cars. I don't get to do that where I am."

Jude could only chuckle as May jumped up and down in obvious excitement. "Oh my god," she cried. "I love muscle cars. My brother has an old mustang I'm steal all the time. He always yells at me for taking it but I can't resist, it's such a beautiful car."

Jude stared at her in surprise, then as he watched, her face literally fell. He pushed his chair back and moved towards her.

"Why do you always look so sad when you talk about your brother?" Jude asked, as he wrapped his arms around her.

Jude growled when she looked at Colin before answering. "Don't look at that ass, look at me," he ordered impatiently. Immediately her eyes turned straight back to him.

"I'm sorry," May apologized. "I haven't seen him in a while and I miss him."

"And why haven't you seen him?" Jude questioned.

Colin answered for her. "Long story, and not one we need to get into now. This spaghetti looks great. I've missed your cooking."

May instantly looked pissed. "You've hardly ever had my cooking. You were always too busy."

Colin cleared his throat in embarrassment and shook his head. "Well, I'm not too busy anymore," he practically snarled.

"Knock it the fuck off and eat your spaghetti," Jude growled at the man. Then he pulled out May's chair, helped her sit, and dragged it closer to him.

May giggled as she looked up at him. "It's going to be hard to eat like this," she told him.

"Well, you could eat sitting on my lap instead?" Jude offered. He threw back his head and laughed when she actually tilted her head and considered it.

"Okay, maybe that's not a good idea," he smirked. "You'll distract me too much."

Jude then turned to his plate and dug in. As soon as he swallowed he turned to a May. "Best fucking spaghetti ever," he declared after he'd swallowed. Then he proceeded to wolf it down. When he looked over at May, and passed her his empty plate, she smiled at him.

"More?" Jude requested. Then her smile got bigger as she filled it again. When he looked over at Colin, it surprised him to see the man's plate was still half full.

"Quit being a pansy and eat like a man," Jude teased him. He laughed when Colin narrowed his eyes at him.

After they finished dinner, May cleared the dishes away, then dragged them outside to sit on the front porch. It was still early, and the night was warm. They sat in silence for quite a while until the roar of motorcycles could be heard in the distance. When they looked up, three Harley's and a truck came down the road.

Jude stood and headed for them, but Colin held May back. "You know them?" he questioned her.

Jude immediately stopped and glared at the man for the hundredth time that evening. "They're friends of mine," he growled at the ass. Then he watched as Navaho, Sniper and Raid climbed off the bikes and Dagger climbed out of the truck.

"No," Dagger complained. "She's wearing a fucking dress. I miss the tee shirt."

Jude shook his head as he turned to Colin, but the man was already glaring at May. "You're moving somewhere else."

Jude went to yell at the fucker again, but Dagger was faster.

"Fuck that," he sneered. "She just got here." Then he turned to May. "Who's the stuffed shirt in the suit, you need us to make him disappear?"

"Fucking Dagger," Jude snorted, as May giggled, and Colin looked ready to blow.

Chapter 16
Jude

Jude looked over at Colin as the bikers pulled up and grinned when he saw the man looked ready to blow. Dagger's lewd comments were definitely making things worse. He shook his head as he headed over to them

"Hey guys, what brings you here?" Jude questioned to distract the bikers. Navaho lifted his chin in greeting, then headed to the back of the truck.

"Brought some wood. Thought we'd fix the steps. Don't want you stuck in them again," Navaho replied with as little words as possible. Behind him, he heard May snicker. The girl still stood on the porch and looked amused by the scene in front of her.

"May already fixed it," Jude helpfully told the bikers. "She painted it yellow."

"That's temporary," May defended. But all Jude could do was grin at her.

"Right, I don't think you and a hammer would get along well together," Jude chuckled. "We'd need Doc on standby if you tried that one."

"I can fix a stupid step without hurting myself," she argued back with a slight frown.

"Yep," Jude agreed sarcastically. "I've seen you with a ladder and a curtain rod. I've seen you moving furniture. Oh, but the best was you wrestling with the shower curtain."

"Shut up Lucy," May immediately yelled at him. "That was because my water heater broke," she complained.

"Don't call me Lucy," Jude growled in agitation.

"I can look at that for you sweetheart," Raid interrupted.

"Don't call her sweetheart," Jude yelled at Raid as he turned to glare at the biker.

Dagger choice that moment to throw back his head and laugh. "You two are better than the fucking detectives," he declared. "And the things they come out with always fucking crack me up."

"Tripp's a fucking brother now," Navaho admonished. "Keep him out of this."

"Righty hoe, Navaho," Dagger responded. Then he yelped and hid behind Sniper as the biker took a threatening step towards him.

May was giggling as she skipped down the steps, with Colin right on her heels.

"I really don't like this," Jude heard Colin complain. "Bikers aren't good people," the ass argued.

"Hey," Jude yelled at him furiously, pissed at the man's attitude towards his friends. "What the fucks the problem with bikers?"

"Nothing, it's just May's a quiet person, and likes to be by herself," Colin replied.

When Jude looked at May, she was staring at the ground, and looked sad again. He remembered the night he asked her to turn down her music, and she told him she hated the quiet because she was used to having all her brother's friends around. What Colin said contradicted that.

"Hey, Raid, Sniper, come over here for a second will you," Jude called. When the bikers were close, he turned back to Colin. "Colin here's a friend of May's. He has concerns about the type of people she hangs around. Care to tell him what you did for a living?" he asked.

Sniper turned to Colin and smirked, figuring out immediately what Jude was getting at. "I was a sniper for the marine corp," Sniper informed the ass. "Raid here was my spotter. Shadow, another biker, was special forces, and Tripp was a detective. You need not worry about May's safety," Sniper assured the man.

Colin raised his eyebrows. "Well then, I apologize," the ass responded sincerely. Both bikers gave him a minute, then nodded in acceptance.

"And I specialize in dynamite," Dagger added cutting into the conversation. "I like to blow shit up."

The bikers laughed. "He's fucking good at that. Blew up a whole house about three months ago," Sniper informed them, then he turned and headed for the porch steps while Colin gaped at him.

Jude chuckled as he headed to the back of the truck to help Navaho with the wood and tools.

"He really a friend?" Navaho questioned quietly.

"Yep," Jude replied. "He's friends with her brother, but he's got cop written all over him. Be good if Tripp suddenly showed, he'd be able to tell us for sure."

Navaho nodded, then moved away to make the call. "Brother can be here in five," he said when he returned a minute later.

"Appreciated," Jude told him. Then they carried everything back to the porch. May squealed, when Raid and Sniper went back to the truck and pulled out a beautiful blue steel door.

"You got me a new door," she cried happily as she clapped her hands.

"What happened to your old door?" Colin asked, as he ran his hands through his hair in frustration.

"Jude ran through it," May happily supplied. "His muscles came out again."

Colin raised his brow, but didn't bother asking, and Jude figured the fucker was finally giving up.

"What can I help with?" Colin sighed, and May sent a smile his way. Jude was happy to see she was losing the sad expression she'd worn for the last couple hours.

Jude decided he would have to do some digging, things were getting real interesting with May. First thing tomorrow he'd give Mario a call. If anyone could find something out, that man could.

Chapter 17
May

May sat on the porch and watched happily as the bikers, along with Jude and Colin, fixed her steps and replaced her door. She loved the blue colour of the door and thought it brightened up the tiny house. She couldn't stop watching Jude as he worked though and basically ignored everyone else. He was sweating, and his damp shirt was sticking to his muscular chest.

Just after they started working, another member of the biker club showed up. May had been told his name was Tripp, and before he joined their ranks he was a detective. Tripp quickly introduced himself to Colin, then seemed to glue himself to her friend for the rest of the evening. She discreetly moved closer and caught some of their conversation.

"So I hear you're a banker?" Tripp casually inquired.

"And I hear your an ex-cop," Colin had replied.

"Yep," Tripp immediately confirmed. "I was a beat cop before I made detective."

Colin eyed him curiously as he frowned. "So why did you quit?" he questioned, when Tripp offered no more information.

"I was getting sick of the job. It seemed like no matter what I did, the damn paperwork got in the way. Then my girl got into trouble and I couldn't help her because of all the red tape. When The Stone Knight's asked me to join I jumped on board. It was with their help I got my girl out of her mess," Tripp explained to Colin.

"So you chose the illegal route?" Colin questioned rudely while sneering at the man.

"No," Tripp replied with barely restrained patience. "I chose the route that would stop the fucker that was messing with her from taking his knife and slicing her again. He cut her hand and cut up her side, but there was no way to stop it legally. Would you watch someone you care about get hurt and not do anything about it?" Tripp asked.

Colin stared at the biker a minute, then he looked at May. "I understand. Sometimes the law hinders us more than it helps us. I get the need to take matters into your own hands. It's painful to watch people you care about get hurt right in front of your eyes."

Finally Colin looked away from her, and it broke the tension surrounding them. But his words had affected her deeply. She knew that seeing her and her brother get hurt had been hard for the man. She moved to him and placed her hand on his arm in support. He nodded at her and sighed.

"There something we should know Colin?" Tripp asked as he studied her friend closely. Colin ruffled her hair and moved away, and she hated the fake smile he conveniently plastered on his face.

"Nope," Colin replied a little too quickly. "But, I'll let you know if a problem arises where I ever need your help." Then he turned back to her and smiled softly for real this time.

"It's time for me to go squirt," Colin eventually admitted, causing pain to radiate from her chest. May nodded sadly, knowing he shouldn't have even come.

"I know," May told him. "Will you come back soon, maybe bring the boys?" she practically begged.

"We'll see," was all Colin would tell her. "Is there anything you want me to tell them?" he inquired. She nodded, then turned and ran into the house. She moved to her nightstand and pulled out the letter she had written to her brother. Grinning, she ran back out the door and hurried down the steps. Then she shoved it in Colin's hand and gave him a tight hug.

"Be careful," May whispered into his ear as he squeezed her back just as tightly.

"Stay safe," Colin whispered back. "I'll be in touch when I can." She didn't say a word, just watched sadly as he climbed in his car and drove away.

That was when Jude came up to her and wrapped his big arms around her from behind. The bikers were still scattered across the lawn and were now eyeing her curiously. She was sure that after seeing her and Colin together they had questions. Somehow she knew they had been listening to the entire conversation Colin had with Tripp.

"You want to tell me what that was about?" Jude ordered with a bite to his words. May immediately pulled out of his arms and plastered a fake smile on her face. She turned to face the bikers instead of answering.

"Thank you so much for helping me with my house. It means a lot you took the time to do this for me." Then she turned to Jude. "Thanks for coming to dinner, I loved having you here." Then before anyone could reply she hurried up the steps and stood in the door, while everyone stared at her like she was a nut.

"I'm tired, so I'll see you around," May announced, as she shut and locked the door on them all.

Chapter 18
Jude

Jude fumed as May shut the door and clicked the lock. Whenever someone got too inquisitive May shut the conversation down by running away. He let her this time, but only because he needed to talk to the bikers. He shook his head as he twisted to face Tripp.

"Cop," Jude growled in annoyance.

"Definitely," the biker agreed. "At first I thought FBI, but he doesn't appear the type. Most are assholes, this guy seems too down to earth. It's also the way he talks, he talks like a cop and not like a fed," Tripp explained.

"What about your speech about Fable?" Jude questioned curiously.

"That was to feel him out," Tripp admitted. "When he told us he knew what it felt like he was looking at May with a deep sadness. I'd bet my ass he's protecting her from something. I can try to look into it, but you may have more luck with Mario," Tripp explained.

"I was thinking the same thing," Jude agreed. "And I don't want to put Darren in a bad position."

"Should we break her door down and carry her away?" Dagger asked, completely serious.

"No fucker," Jude growled. "We give her the night to cool off."

"You want a brother on her house?" Navaho questioned.

"If you can spare it I'd appreciate it," Jude huffed.

Navaho nodded, then turned to make the call.

"Call Mario," Sniper ordered as he tied up the tools he had been using. "Fucker can work magic." Jude nodded and pulled out his cell, placing the call.

"Mario," the man answered on the first ring.

"Jude here," Jude told him right away.

"Jude, been a week since I saw you. You doing good?" Mario asked.

"I am," Jude replied. "But I'd be doing better if I found out what the fuck my girl's got herself into," he admitted. Mario instantly lost his casual tone and turned all business.

"Talk to me," he demanded.

"Girl seems to be running from something. I'm sure the name she's using isn't her real name, and a cop came by today. He's a friend, but some things he said caught my attention," Jude told the man.

"You bringing the Knight's in on this?" Mario inquired.

"They're already in, who the fuck do you think pushed me to make the call?" Jude sneered. Mario chuckled on the other end.

"Right," he replied. "I'm free for a beer tonight at the clubhouse. You free in about an hour?" Mario asked.

"Sounds good," Jude answered without hesitation. "I'll be there."

They hung up and Jude had to admit he felt better. "Mario will be at the clubhouse shortly," he told the bikers gathered around him.

"Great," Dagger smirked. "I'll get the dynamite."

"No dynamite," they all yelled at him at once.

"But there's always dynamite when a girl is in trouble," Dagger pouted.

"We don't even know what we're dealing with," Sniper said as he glared at the biker. "Hold the fuck off for a while."

"Okay, so I'll go stock pile for later," Dagger grinned, as he headed for his bike.

"That ass will kill himself one day," Raid chuckled.

"Probably," Jude agreed, shaking his head.

The men cleaned up the tools they'd brought and put away the rest of the supplies. The bikers said their goodbyes then headed to the clubhouse, while Jude headed to his house to change. Once done, he marched back over to May's house and pounded on the door.

As soon as she opened the door Jude pulled her into his chest, wrapped his arms around her, and dropped his lips down on hers. She stood stiff for a minute, then melted into the kiss. Jude gave it his all and put all his frustrations into it. He deepened it and bent her over slightly as she clung to him. Finally, when he felt the need to breathe, he broke away.

Staring down at her, Jude saw the familiar dazed expression he was getting used to after they shared a kiss. He smirked, placed a soft kiss on her nose, and let her go. Then he turned and started across the lawn to his bike. When he reached it he turned, to see she was still standing in the doorway, watching him warily.

"Don't ever fucking slam and lock a door on me again," he yelled. Then he climbed on his bike and pulled out of the drive. He didn't look back once as he tore off for the compound.

Chapter 19
Jude

Jude pulled through the gates of The Stone Knight's compound and backed his bike into line beside the others already parked there. Jude loved hanging out with the bikers, but today was more business than pleasure. He was happy to see Mario's sleek black car was already there. He shut down his bike, climbed off, and headed inside.

Immediately, Jude saw Mario and his right-hand man Trent sitting at a table with Steele, Tripp, Dragon, Navaho, Shadow and Sniper. He pulled out a chair beside Navaho and took a seat.

"Where's Dagger," Jude questioned with amusement. "I thought for sure the brother would be here for this."

"We locked him in his room," Navaho grinned. "Figured he'd say something dumb, and we'd only have to cart his ass there anyway. Saves time this way."

Jude chuckled as he shook his head. "Smart," he admitted.

Tripp immediately got down to business. "I know May's friend is named Colin, but I didn't get a last name. I did however get a licence plate, and I'm positive he's a cop," he explained, as he slid a piece of paper across the table to Mario. Mario immediately passed it to Trent, who had a pad of paper in front of him.

"Do we have a last name for May?" Mario inquired.

Jude sighed. "She never said, but we've never really gotten that far," he admitted.

"Name is May North," Tripp supplied, causing Jude's head to snap up.

"How the fuck do you know that?" Jude asked.

Tripp smirked. "I was a detective until about two months ago. Her car keys were laying on the counter, and the key-chain had her name on it."

Mario nodded. "Okay, any parents or siblings?"

"Never mentioned any parents, but she talks about a brother all the time. Hasn't seen him in a while, don't know why though," Jude added. "She also mentioned that she moved from up north, but that leaves it pretty open."

Tripp slid another piece of paper across the table. "This is her licence plate," he declared. Trent placed it with the other one, as he continued to write stuff on his pad.

Suddenly a crash came from down the hall where the rooms were located.

Steele chuckled. "Fucker broke out," he told them. Jude turned to the hall and watched as Dagger trotted out and headed towards them.

"Four nails?" Dagger smirked. "That's the best you can do? Last time you propped a chair under the door, even that was harder."

"My turn next time," Dragon chuckled as he rubbed his hands together. "I'll get creative."

Dagger turned and gave the biker the finger. Once the laughing died down Snake came over with a tray of beers and placed them in the middle of the table.

He didn't say a word afterwards, just turned and left. Jude picked one up and took a long pull, savouring the bitter taste.

"She's got a burner phone," Jude added after a minute. "She missed a call the other day, and when she went to her contacts, I noticed she only had two."

"Anything else you can think of?" Mario asked.

"She lives in a shit house, she drives a shit car, and she has nothing personal in her space," Shadow interrupted. "Girl can leave in a fucking hurry if she needs to."

"Shit," Jude cursed, pissed he didn't catch that. "I just fucking met her, if she runs I'll never find her." He was furious, and he didn't know how he would handle it if she left.

"I got some ideas on how you can keep her here," Dagger smirked, as he tipped his chair and leaned back casually.

"Fuck off," Jude answered automatically.

Dagger got angry then and his chair slammed back to the floor. "You know, not everything I say is a god damned joke. Hear me the fuck out," he ordered.

Stunned, Jude and the rest of the bikers stared at him.

"Pull some wires on her car, then offer to have it towed to the garage here. No fast getaway," Dagger snickered. "Damage her roof, then offer to let her stay with you. Scare the shit out of her, move some branches so they tap at her window all night. Or you could dump a cup of ants in her house, and again she'd need to stay with you," he advised. "Start small, just piss her off so you have excuses to get her into your house all the time."

"God dammit," Jude declared with some relief. "You're a fucking genius."

"See fuckers," Dagger grinned proudly. "Not just a pretty face."

Chapter 20
May

May was laying in bed later that night, but she just couldn't seem to fall asleep. It had crushed her to see Colin leave, even though she was incredibly pissed off at him. He always treated her like a little sister, and not once had he treated her any differently until tonight. And he'd never told her she looked pretty before. He had actually acted like a jealous ass at dinner, and that wasn't right.

May thought of Jude and the way he treated her. Sure he seemed to always be annoyed with her, but even when she first met him, they had a chemistry that was hard to resist. She also secretly loved the caveman routine. It thrilled May to have a guy that was possessive of her, it made her feel special. It also made her feel wanted, and she needed that right now.

She turned towards her window and fumed. There was a tree growing up outside, and the stupid branches were scratching the glass. At first it had just annoyed her, but now it was scaring her half to death. It sounded like someone was outside and trying to get in, and it creeped her out. It felt too close to what could actually happen.

After about ten minutes more she'd had enough. It had never done this until tonight, and she couldn't take it anymore. She threw back the covers, climbed out of bed, and pulled on a pair of sweat pants. Grabbing her glasses, she stomped through the house. She unlocked and pushed open the back door, then headed outside. It was warm but breezy, which explained why the branches were moving so much tonight.

May rounded the house and headed straight for the tree. The street light gave her enough light to see, so she didn't need a flashlight. It didn't take her long to spot the branches that were scratching her window. She stared in utter disbelief. It looked like the branches had been twisted and positioned to hit her window, which made little sense.

Pissed now, May moved towards the closest one and pulled with everything she had. The stupid branch moved, but didn't come unstuck. The other two branches were just above her head, and too far away to reach. She tried jumping, but that didn't work at all. Eyeing the branches warily, she decided she hated how short she was.

Then May eyed the tree trunk curiously and studied it for a minute. The trunk was thick, and there were lots of lower hanging branches sticking out. May had grown up with a brother, he had taught her early on how to climb trees, and this one looked fairly easy. She headed straight to the trunk and grabbed onto the lowest branch. Then she placed one bare foot on the trunk and climbed with her feet. Finally she could wrap her legs around the tree and pull the rest of her body up. After a quick spin, she was sitting comfortably on the branch.

May searched the tree for the branches she was looking for. It didn't take long to follow the annoying scratching sound and locate them. She had to climb up higher to reach them, but that didn't bother her. Once she was stable, she grabbed one of the branches and pulled with everything she had. And again the damn thing wouldn't move. Huffing angrily, she gave up and climbed back down. Because she was so small, she didn't have the strength she needed to bend them.

May stomped back across the lawn and headed into the kitchen. She didn't have a saw, but she had a really sharp butcher knife. Without thought, she grabbed it and headed back outside. Eyeing the tree again, she reached up and slammed the knife in a thick branch. Then she hauled herself up to where she was previously and pulled the knife back out.

May eyed the branch and shimmied out as far as she could, then placed the blade against the limb and hacked away at it. After what felt like hours she cheered as the limb gave way and fell to the ground. She shimmied back to the trunk, located the second branch, and shimmied out on that one next. Then again, she started to hack away at it.

"What in the ever loving fuck do you think you're doing?" was roared from the direction of Jude's house.

May jumped in fright, dropping the knife she'd been holding. She cursed a blue streak, then watched in horror as the branch she was perched on cracked. But it didn't crack where she was cutting, the branch cracked at the trunk. The pressure of her jumping in fright must have been too much for it. She screamed as the branch broke off and fell to the ground, with her still sitting on it.

Chapter 21
Jude

Jude headed straight home after the meeting at the compound. It wasn't late, so he snuck over to May's and peeked in her windows. He felt like a peeping Tom, but he ignored that thought and continued with the plan.

Jude checked the living room first, and when he discovered it was empty, he headed around the house to her bedroom. When he peeked in and saw it was empty too, he grinned as he headed for the bathroom. The window was frosted over, so he couldn't see in, but he could hear the water running. His pretty little klutz was in the shower.

Jude hurried back to her bedroom window and sized up the tree that was growing beside it. After looking it over for a minute, he decided it wouldn't be too difficult to muscle a couple of the branches so they hit her window. Smiling, he decided it was time to put Dagger's plan into action.

It took Jude ten minutes to maneuver the branches in just the right position, and he was sweating by the time he was done. He smiled at his handiwork, patted himself on the back, and headed back over to his own place. Jude couldn't wait for May to come knocking on his door, terrified of the scratching noise. He unlocked his door, grabbed a beer, and sat down.

An hour later, Jude headed to bed, hoping she was in bed as well. He tried not to fall asleep too deeply, because he wanted to hear her when she knocked. But minutes later he was sound to the world, despite what he had wanted.

Something woke Jude a while later, and it took him a minute to wake completely. Figuring it had to be his klutz, he happily climbed off the bed, and headed to the front door. He had on his sleep pants, but left off the tee, so he opened the door with a smile, hoping she liked what she saw.

When Jude looked out, it surprised him to see there was no one there. He poked his head out and looked left then right, but May was nowhere to be seen.

Jude scratched his head in confusion, sure a knock on the door had woken him.

He couldn't help tilting his head and listening, trying to hear something to let him know what woke him. Finally he heard faint little grunts coming from in between the houses. He immediately headed out the door and around the house, curious to see what she was up to.

Jude assumed she was trying to physically move the branches, and was about to chuckle, but when he looked for her she wasn't there. Stunned, he searched around, but there was absolutely no sign of her. Although, he saw there was a branch lying on the ground. Then he heard her cute little grunts again, and his eyes followed the sound.

Jude about blew a gasket when he located her sitting in the god damned tree, and sawing at a branch. His klutz wasn't following the plan. She was supposed to come to him for help, not climb the god damned thing in her pyjamas and cut it down. Throwing his hands up in the air in frustration, he yelled at her without thinking it through first.

Jude realized right away it was the wrong thing to do, and watched in absolute horror as the branch broke and came down, with her on top of it. Her scream was enough to terrify him, and he took off at a dead run for the tree.

When he reached her, he fell on his knees beside her, and stared down at her in panic. Her eyes were closed, and that scared him.

"Jesus May," he frantically yelled. "Open your eyes," Jude demanded as he searched for a pulse. Immediately his hand was smacked away.

"I'm not dead you idiot," May huffed. "The tree wasn't that tall." Then as he watched, her eyes popped open and she slowly sat up. "I only closed my eyes because I didn't want to see myself fall."

He stared at the sky for a minute, praying for patience, before grabbing her under the arms and hauling her to her feet. As soon as she was standing, she yelped and lifted her right foot off the ground.

Fucking great he groaned, not only had his plan backfired, but he'd unintentionally hurt her.

Chapter 22
May

Jude held onto her as she lifted her foot off the ground. It hurt, but May knew it wasn't broken. She turned to hobble into the house, but he scooped her up and marched around to the back door. He shifted her in his arms, pulled the door open, and stomped inside. A second later, she was deposited on the couch.

"What the hell were you doing in that tree?" Jude demanded.

May sighed in agitation. "A couple branches were scratching at the window, and it gave me the creeps," she admitted. As she watched, he paced back and forth across her living room.

"So you climbed the damned thing and cut them off?" Jude yelled.

May narrowed her eyes at him. "Yes," she yelled back. "I couldn't reach them, what was I supposed to do?"

Jude stopped then and turned to her, and she could see the temper he was trying to tamper down. "Maybe come get me," he growled.

She blinked as she looked at him. "Whatever for?" she asked in confusion.

Jude huffed, and she had to bite her lip to keep from laughing. "So I could help you," he pushed.

It was then she noticed his bare chest. The man was built like a linebacker, and he had several tattoos. She stared at them, trying to figure out what they were.

"May," Jude shouted, causing her eyes to snap back to his. "Are you even listening?"

"Nope," she admitted right away. "You don't have a shirt on."

He threw his hands up in the air. "What does that have to do with anything?" he questioned.

"It's a very nice chest," she said, as she went back to staring at it.

"Jesus May," Jude huffed. "Eyes up here."

She giggled, as she completely ignored him. His chest was fascinating, she'd rather keep looking at it.

She heard him sigh, then he was pulling out his phone and making a call.

"Navaho, Doc still up?" Jude asked. "Good, cart his ass over here." Then, he paused. "She fucking climbed the tree and tried to saw the branches off with a kitchen knife." Even through the phone, she could hear Navaho's laughter.

"Fuck off," Jude sneered, then he hung up the phone. "Doc will be here in a minute," he told her as he pocketed it.

True enough, ten minutes later, Doc and Navaho pushed through the door and she sighed in relief. "Thank god," May said from her perch on the couch. "He's wearing down my floor. Can you make him sit somewhere?" she begged the men.

Jude turned to her and scowled. "I'm pissed at you," he growled. "Trying to cut a tree branch with a kitchen knife, what the hell were you thinking?"

"Hey," May yelled. "It was working until you came along. Besides, now it gives me an excuse to buy a saw." Then she tilted her head in thought as she considered her options. "Or maybe a hatchet."

Navaho threw back his head and roared. "You got your work cut out for you with this one," he told Jude.

May snickered then turned to Doc. "Can you check my ankle so those two asses can leave," she pleaded. Doc smiled and did as she asked, poking and prodding at it. A minute later he looked up at her.

"Just a slight strain," he explained. "Keep it up, ice it on and off, and you'll be good as new in a couple days."

May smiled gratefully. "Thanks Doc." Then she stood, hopped to the freezer, and opened the door.

"What the ever loving fuck are you doing?" Jude roared obviously upset about something else.

She spun to glare at him. "Look Lucy," May huffed. "It's been a long day and I'm tired. Doc said I need to ice it, so that's what I'm doing. And you can't yell at me because I hopped, I didn't walk on it," she told him, figuring that's what he would mention.

"On that note, we're out of here," Navaho chuckled, as he and Doc took off out the door.

"You need to come stay with me," Jude ordered, as he crossed his arms over his chest.

May blinked at him in surprise. "Why?" she questioned, as she removed the ice, and hopped to the dish towel that was on the side of the stove.

"Will you stop fucking doing that," Jude roared. Then she screeched as he picked her up and carried her back to the couch. A minute later ice was placed on her ankle.

"You never do what normal people would do," he sighed, then he pulled her into his arms and held the ice gently on her ankle.

Chapter 23
Jude

Jude had no idea what to do with his pretty little klutz. The tree plan had certainly backfired on him. He didn't understand how she could think going out and trying to cut it down herself was a good idea. Although she was like no other woman he had known, so of course she would do what no other woman would.

Jude sat with her curled up tight against his chest, as he held the ice on her foot. He was damn lucky she hadn't hurt herself more. When she fell, and he saw her eyes were closed, he thought he'd killed her for sure. He was sure his heart actually stopped for a minute. May shifted, and when he looked down, she was staring up at him.

"I'm exhausted, I think I'll head back to bed now," she told him as she yawned. Jude nodded, then stood with her and carried her down the hall to her bedroom. As gently as he could, he laid her on the bed and pulled the sheets up to her chest.

"I'm staying with you tonight," he demanded. "So don't god damned argue with me," he quickly said before she could get a word in.

"Okay Lucy," replied as she yawned again and curled into the pillow.

"Fuck me," Jude said, as he grabbed the towel that held the ice and left the room. His girl was cute when she was tired.

Jude dumped the ice in the sink, then hung the towel up in the bathroom to dry. He wanted to get her to ice it again in the morning, so he'd need the towel dry. Next, he pushed out the back door and headed for the tree. When he saw the tree, he stood there in stunned silence.

Someone had chopped every branch that was anywhere near her bedroom window off. There was no way, even in a hurricane, that any branches would get anywhere near it. Someone had taken great care to make sure May never had to get near that tree again.

Jude headed to his house, grabbed his cell, and made sure it was secure. Then he trooped back across the lawn and stopped just before he reached the back door. He pulled out his cell, hit a button, and placed it against his ear.

"Jude," he heard in greeting.

"Navaho," he greeted in return. "Appreciate the tree trimming," he told the biker.

Navaho chuckled in his ear. "Well, we don't need her hopping out in the morning to finish the fucking job," he laughed.

"No, and she fucking would too," Jude sighed.

"You get her over to your place yet," Navaho asked.

"Nope, but in all honesty, I didn't have the heart to push that on her tonight. I'll wait until the morning to get back to that," Jude replied.

Navaho chuckled again. "Right. Get some sleep," he ordered. "You'll need to be on top of your game tomorrow." Then he listened as the biker ended the call by hanging up.

Jude huffed, as he powered off his phone and shoved it in his pocket. Then he was pushing open the back door to head back into May's. He did a sweep of the place and made sure it was locked up tight, then headed to her bedroom.

The girl was sound asleep, and was hugging the extra pillow tight to her chest. Jude placed all his crap on her nightstand, then carefully climbed on the bed. As gently as he could, he maneuvered the pillow out of her arms and placed it back at the top of the bed. Then he got comfortable and slid his arms under her so he could drag her over so she was tight to his side. He chuckled as she curled into him more and laid her tiny head on his shoulder.

Jude stared at the ceiling and thought about his pretty little klutz. He decided he was keeping her. He didn't care what trouble she was in, she wasn't going anywhere. He'd fix it, and he'd make everything okay for her. In his arms was where she was meant to be, and he would make sure she stayed there. He fell asleep a little while later with a smile on his face, and a determination in his heart. His girl had no idea what conclusion he had just come to, but it didn't matter, because she didn't have a choice anyway.

Chapter 24
May

Warmth surrounded May, and the room was
completely quiet. She wondered who finished
cutting down the tree branches, because she never
got the chance to go back out and do it herself. She
snuggled into Jude's chest and sighed in
contentment. It had been either him or Navaho, and
she was betting it was Navaho. Jude had been too
quick to accomplish that, when he went to his house
for those few minutes.

May sighed as she thought about Jude. She really
liked him, but this was a temporary situation, and she
didn't want him or the bikers hurt. Maybe when all
this was over she could come back and see if they
could continue what they were starting.

She tried to move, but the handsome ass had his arm tight around her waist. She pulled at it, but the damn thing wouldn't budge. The bathroom was calling, and May needed to move. She slid her hand up and ticked his armpit. Jude immediately screeched a blue moon and let her go.

"What the fuck did you do that for?" he questioned her sleepily. May grinned as she shrugged at him.

"You wouldn't move, and I have to go to the bathroom," she admitted. He didn't reply, just frowned at her.

"You could have just asked me," he scowled.

"Duh, you were asleep. Besides, my way was a lot more fun," she giggled. Then she kneed him in the chest as she climbed over him and scooted off the bed. He grunted and grabbed her before her foot hit the floor.

"Stop fucking walking on that thing," Jude snarled.

May blinked as she looked down at him. "But I need to use the bathroom." Then she squealed as he picked her up, climbed off the bed, and carried her into the bathroom. He then dumped her on the counter.

"Thanks Lucy," she said sarcastically, as she slipped off and pushed the door shut. In minutes she had everything done she needed and was opening the door and hopping back into the room.

Jude was there immediately, picking her up again, and carting her to the couch. When he set her down, she glared up at him.

"Don't you have stuff to do?" she asked him angrily.

"Nope," the ass admitted. "I'm free all day to cart you around. I'm thinking I should just cart you to my house, and you can rest there for a couple days."

"And I'm thinking your delusional," she returned. "Go home, take a couple pills, and call me when you feel better," she ordered. "I have stuff to do, and you're in the way."

Again he glared at her. "What's the matter with staying at my place?" he asked.

"Nothing," May lied through her teeth. "But I have a canvas calling my name, and it's something I can do while I sit around," she explained.

"You paint?" Jude questioned in surprise.

"No," she told him. "I use pastels. It's messier, but I love the way the finished piece turns out. I play my music and just loose complete track of time," she admitted.

"Where are your supplies?" he asked curiously.

"In the hall closet," May told him. Instantly, he was up and making trips back and forth to retrieve everything she'd need.

"Thank you?" she said when he was done.

"You don't have an easel," Jude told her as he scratched his head.

"No, I like to sit on the floor, which will work out well for me today," May smirked.

"Can I see some of your work?" he asked. Her shoulders slumped, as she looked down at the floor sadly.

"I left it all behind," she told him quietly.

Jude studied her for a minute, and she shifted nervously under his gaze. Then he nodded and walked towards her. Kneeling down, he placed his hands on either side of her face and kissed her softly.

She couldn't resist melting into him. When he pulled back, she could only stare at him.

"Fine," Jude announced. "You do your thing, but I'll be back at lunch with burgers. You do like burgers right?" he asked as he headed to the door. She nodded like an idiot, then watched as he smirked before leaving.

May hated the thought of walking away from him, but she would need to do it. Although, it could wait a couple days more she thought to herself.

Chapter 25
Jude

Jude went to the garage he worked at on The Stone Knight's compound for a couple hours. There was a car he wanted to finish in the next day or so, and he still had a bit of work left to do on it. Of course, not long after he arrived Dragon and Trike cornered him.

"Navaho said you attempted to freak out your girl with a tree," Trike chuckled. "I heard it didn't go so well."

Jude sighed. "It's my own fault for listening to Dagger in the first place," he admitted.

"Nah," Dragon denied. "Dagger's plan was solid, it's just your girls a nut," he smirked.

Jude glared at the biker. "May's not a nut," he growled. "She just takes care of things herself."

"She climbed a tree in the middle of the night and tried to saw off the branches with a butcher knife. She's a nut," Dragon chuckled.

Jude hung his head in defeat. "Fine," he conceded. "But she's a fucking pretty nut."

"You moved her in yet?" Trike questioned.

"No," Jude admitted. "She wouldn't budge. I'm fucking frustrated. How the fuck do I keep her safe, if I can't get her to stay with me?"

"Move in with her then genius," Sniper interrupted, as he walked through the door. "Don't give her a choice."

"Are you kidding?" Jude asked.

"Fuck no," Sniper said. "Your girl needs protection, you don't fuck around. Move your ass in and keep her safe."

Jude stood there flabbergasted. "Fuck me, your right," he grinned. "Why the hell didn't I think of that?"

"Because you're not thinking straight right now. You're so set on getting her in your place, you're not considering other options," Sniper acknowledged.

"When the fuck did you become Dr. Phil?" Dragon asked.

"Fuck off," Sniper told the biker. "Priorities change, and you see things differently when your girl tries to kill your sister and bury her in a mine."

"Fuck, sorry brother," Dragon apologized.

Sniper nodded at him. "I didn't get to my sister until it was almost too late. Thank fuck Trike stepped in and was there when I wasn't. If you even have an inkling that your girls in trouble, you do everything you can to make sure she stays safe," he growled. Then the biker turned and walked right back out the door.

"Jesus," Trike sneered. "Carly fucked him up a lot more than I thought. He needs a girl that's so in love with him she can't see straight. Someone that can heal him and make him forget that bitch."

"I hope that girl shows up soon, he deserves to be happy," Dragon added. Then he turned to Jude. "It's almost lunch time, take off and head to May's. Don't worry about the car, we'll get it sorted."

Jude nodded. "Appreciated," he replied. "I told May I'd pick her up a burger for lunch. Now I have to figure out how to pack a bag and explain to her why I'm moving in."

"Easy, use one of Dagger's suggestions. Tell her you got ants, you need some place to stay while it's being fumigated," Trike suggested.

"That could work," Jude decided, as he seriously considered the idea.

"Keep us posted," Dragon chuckled. "And call if you need us."

"Will do," Jude agreed as he headed for his motorcycle.

As soon as he reached it, his phone rang.

"Jude," he said as he answered it.

"It's Mario," was the reply he got. "I ran Colin's plates. Names Colin Snow and he's a cop up north. May's plates are listed under his grandmothers name. I ran May's name, but as we assumed, I got nothing. Girl doesn't exist. I have some friends up there digging into Colin's cases to see if anything is connected to May. I also have them checking into his friends. If he's known her as long as they say, they should be able to find her or her brother. I hope to know within a day or two," Mario advised him.

"Well this just got worse," Jude growled. "It's obvious now she's hiding and doesn't want to be found."

"My friends will be discreet. May will be safe. We'll make sure no one know's where she is," Mario promised. "Didn't get this far by being sloppy."

"Never doubted it," Jude snorted. "I'll wait to hear."

"Right. Keep your girl safe," Mario ordered as he hung up.

Jude started his motorcycle and headed to the burger joint. His girl was getting a roommate, and he wasn't taking no for an answer.

Chapter 26
May

May worked hard all morning on her canvas. She loved the yellow colour of her walls, and so she decided just to do a colourful abstract to hang in the room. It was bright and beautiful, and even though it was only half done, she was already in love with it.

She'd gotten up only twice since she started. Once was to use the bathroom, and the other time was to get a drink. Each time she had glanced all around her, making sure the handsome ass wasn't lurking. She wouldn't put it past him to be lying in wait somewhere, just so he could pop out and yell at her again.

Hours had passed since Jude had left, but May barely noticed. She was immersed in her work and loving every minute. She ignored her growling stomach and picked up a bright blue pastel. No matter how many canvases she worked on, blue was always a prominent colour in them.

When the front door opened May jumped, not realizing someone was close. Her glasses slid down her nose, and she scrambled to push them up before they fell off completely.

"Jesus Lucy, don't you knock?" she gasped, as she breathed in and out and willed her heart to slow down.

"I did," he replied as he frowned down at her. "And you need to learn to lock that door when you're home alone," he growled. She blinked at him in stunned silence, then shrugged. "And don't call me Lucy," he ordered.

She grinned, then stretched and attempted to get up.

"Don't you fucking dare stand on that ankle," Jude yelled. Dutifully, she plopped back down. He nodded happily and dropped a paper bag on her coffee table. Then he shrugged a huge duffle bag off his back and dropped it to the floor.

"What, are you moving in?" May teased him.

"Yep," he confirmed as he took two containers of fries, and two burgers out of the bags.

She chuckled. "I'm sorry, for a minute there I thought you said yes."

"I did," he smirked, as he moved into the kitchen and grabbed two bottles of water.

"No you're not," she huffed, as she placed her hands on her hips. Somehow though it didn't seem quite as intimidating when she was sitting on the floor. She dropped her arms and glared at him instead.

"I've got ants," he declared with a smirk. "So I need to stay here for a while."

"You have ants?" she repeated in amazement.

"Yep," he said, while grinning like a loon. "Big black ones."

May was confused as to what he found so amusing, but she ignored that and powered on.

"So stay with the bikers," she ordered.

"Can't, I'm not a club member," he told her.

"Then get a hotel room," she said as she scrunched up her nose in agitation.

"Nope," Jude shot back, then he headed for her, scooped her up, and plopped her down on the couch. "Jesus, did you get any pastel on the canvas?" he asked, as he frowned down at her. "How the hell did you get it in your hair?"

"Don't change the subject?" May sneered. "You can't stay here."

"You better eat while it's hot," he replied, completely ignoring her comments. "Cold fries suck ass."

"You suck ass," she shot back, as she picked up a fry and went to shove it in her mouth. Jude ripped it out of her hand before she could pop it in.

"Hey," she yelled as her stomach growled.

"Hey back," he repeated. "I think we need to get rid of the blue fry and clean your hands first," he chuckled. "And your nose, and your ears, and you knee, and your..."

"Okay," May agreed, cutting him off. "I get the point." Then she squealed as he picked her up again and carried her into the bathroom. When he placed her on the counter, she looked in the mirror, and sighed. "I tend to get a bit messy."

"It kind of looks cute," he admitted, as he wet a washcloth and started to gently wipe her down. When he was done, he carried her back into the living room and placed her on the couch again. "Eat up my little rainbow bright," he said, as he picked up his burger and took a huge bite.

"You best be thinking about somewhere else to stay while you eat," she advised. "I think the old lady across the street would let you stay with her."

"The cat lady," Jude gasped in horror. "I don't think so."

"Well, you better figure it out," May said, as he grinned at her and continued to eat his burger.

Chapter 27
Jude

After the burgers, Jude lifted May and sat her back on the floor. He loved the pastel art she was doing. She had a talent that was absolutely amazing. She seemed to get lost in her work, and it wasn't long before she completely forgot he was there. That was a perfect opening, he placed his bag in her bedroom and snooped a bit.

May had nothing personal that he could find. No pictures, no jewellery, and not much in terms of belongings. She was definitely in a position to run if she needed too. She could even leave what she had there if it was necessary. And that made him extremely uneasy.

It was getting close to suppertime, but when Jude searched through her fridge and cupboards, he didn't find a lot. He was getting ready to head to the store, when there was a knock on the door. As he watched, May's head snapped up, and she anxiously stared at the door. When Sniper and Raid walked through, she tried unsuccessfully to mask her disappointment.

"We brought dinner?" Sniper greeted, as he held up a couple paper bags. "Hope you like tacos, cause Raid whined until I agreed with him."

"I didn't fucking whine," Raid growled.

"When we got to the chicken place you refused to get off your Harley?" Sniper snickered.

"That's because we had chicken every fucking day in the desert, those fuckers wouldn't know a cow if they saw one," Raid complained. "I need beef."

"You were in the desert?" May asked curiously.

"Yeah, couple years," Sniper explained. "We were in the Marines together."

"That's awesome," May grinned. "My dad was a marine. He died in action."

"I'm sorry," Sniper replied.

Jude watched as May shrugged. "I was young."

"How young?" Jude instantly questioned.

"Nine," she admitted. "It was a long time ago."
Then she changed the subject. "We need plates."
When she went to stand, Jude lost it again.

"Will you fucking stop doing that?" he grumbled.

"Will you stop being a jerk?" she responded.

"You're not supposed to walk on it," Jude growled.
"How is me stopping you from doing that being a
jerk?" he asked in exasperation.

"You could say it a little nicer. Maybe try, please
May, stay where you are and let me help you," she
yelled back at him.

Jude threw up his arms and glared at the ceiling. "By
the time I got all that out you'd be half way across
the room," he huffed.

"I would not," she grumbled.

"You fucking would," he complained. "You're
almost as fast as Trike, and that fuckers fast."

Sniper chuckled and nudged Raid. "I told you this
would be fun."

Jude glared at the bikers, then he moved to the kitchen to get plates and cutlery. Once he had set it on the table, he plucked May off the floor and carried her to the bathroom. Once more he cleaned her up, then carted her back out and set her on a chair.

Dinner was relatively quiet after that. Jude asked Raid about the new bike he was building.

"When do you think it will be done?" Jude asked the biker.

"I'm still waiting for a couple parts to come in," he admitted. Raid had been riding a hand me down, and was exited about building his own. "I'm hoping to have it done by November," he explained.

"What?" May asked as she played with her taco. "I didn't hear what you asked."

Immediately, all three of them stopped eating and stared at her. Jude knew the minute she realized the huge mistake she had just made, because she turned a deathly shade of white.

"November," he said softly. Her head swivelled in his direction. "That's just about the prettiest name I've ever heard," he told her.

Jude didn't say a word, just watched as the different emotions flew across her face. Raid and Sniper silently pushed back their chairs, and left the house. Jude nodded in their direction in silent thanks, and they nodded back. He knew they would pass her real name onto Mario for him.

Now he just had to get her to open up a bit more, because right now she looked ready to bolt, and she'd do it, even if her ankle was fucked up.

Chapter 28
May

May was completely freaked out. She knew she had made a colossal mistake. She should have been listening closer to the conversation. She should never have slipped like that. Jude knew her name, and so did Sniper and Raid. That meant within the hour the entire bike club would know as well. That also meant Tripp would find out, and she knew he was an ex-cop. Her only choice was to backtrack.

"My name is May," she told Jude, as she tried to steady her shaky voice.

"Nice try, but there's no way you can deny it now," Jude softly replied. "Besides, I absolutely love that name. May's such a plain name, November is completely unique. It suits you."

May pushed away from the table and hopped to the door.

"Stop fucking walking on that," Jude growled.

"You need to leave," she demanded as she leaned against the wall. Her head was pounding, and she knew she was on the verge of a panic attack.

Jude stood and shook his head in denial. "I'm not going anywhere my little rainbow."

"You need to leave," she repeated with much more force this time.

"And you need to talk to me," he pushed as he made his way towards her.

"I don't need to do anything," she stubbornly replied as she stared up at him.

"I'm falling in love with you," Jude told her, as he stared down into her eyes. "I've known you such a short time, but I know I belong with you. I can feel you in my heart. I'm not going to lose you."

May suddenly deflated and slid down the wall to sit on the floor. She didn't know what to do, so she did the only thing she could at the moment. She pulled her knees up to her chest, buried her face in them, and cried. Not even a second later, Jude was on the floor beside her, and she was pulled into his strong arms. She shoved her face into his neck, clung to his shirt, and cried harder.

It felt like years since she had cried like this. The stress of everything she was dealing with was becoming too much for her. She had finally reached her breaking point, and she was letting the handsome ass see it. He didn't say a thing, just held her the entire time.

It felt like hours had passed when her tears dried up. May let go of Jude and swiped at them, desperately trying to erase them. Finally, she pulled back and chanced a glance up at him.

"You need to leave," she stubbornly tried again.

"Can't," he smirked. "Ants."

"You're making that up," she accused.

Jude put his hands on his hips. "Did you not see them carry my couch out the front door earlier? Those fuckers are scary big."

"You're just trying to get me to smile," May pouted.

Jude sighed, then placed his arms back around her and pulled her close again. "I am," he told her. "I don't like to see you cry, it breaks something inside me."

May had no reply, and soon he was picking her up and carrying her to the couch. He placed her at one end, then moved down and sat at the other. Confused, she just looked at him.

"You pretty much hit the nail on the head when you called me Lucy," Jude began. "My mom left after I was born, and my dad was a drunk. I grew up stealing and fighting in underground clubs. When I was eighteen, I stole a car. I was caught. Spent two years in jail. The bikers found me after I got out. They gave me a job and helped me sort myself out. I'm a fucking criminal with a record." He stopped and stared at her, so she nodded for him to continue.

"I just wanted to tell you that so you know we all have secrets. When you're ready, you'll tell me yours. And you don't have to worry, I promise to only call you November when we're alone."

Then Jude moved to her and pulled her against him once more, as he settled and clicked on the television. He acted like it was just another normal night after that. Later, when she went to bed, he locked up and joined her. She was almost asleep before she realized what was happening.

"Hey," May whispered drowsily. "You can't stay with me."

"I know little rainbow," he whispered back. Then she fell into an exhausted sleep, with him wrapped tight around her.

Chapter 29
Jude

Jude woke up extremely early. He watched his pretty little rainbow sleep for a few minutes, before he attempted to move. She hadn't showered before going to bed, so she still had pastel in her hair and on her arms. While she slept, it had transferred onto her pillow and sheets. As he glanced down he smirked, realizing he now had a rainbow chest.

After a few minutes, Jude slid out from under her, and carefully placed his pillow where he had been laying. He smiled as he watched her drag it closer and snuggle it. Jude had slept in his sleep pants, so he quickly threw on a tee and hurried from the room. There were a few things he wanted to do, but he wanted to be back in bed before she woke.

Jude slipped down the hall and moved to the closet first. He had seen suitcases in them, and he wanted to deal with them first. He cracked open the door and dragged out the two he had located earlier. In minutes, he had carried them across the yard, and hidden them in his back shed.

Jude slipped back inside and moved to her laundry room next. He knew she kept her garbage bags in there, so he grabbed the box and hurried to the kitchen. Opening the cupboard, he grabbed all the grocery bags she had stored there as well. Then he made his way to the shed again. Once they were hidden with the suitcases, he went back to her house.

Next, Jude moved to her counter. He grabbed her cell and checked her battery. With everything that had happened the night before she had forgotten to charge it, which worked out perfectly. He grabbed her charger and hid it in the back of her cutlery drawer. Then he grabbed her car keys and put them there too.

Satisfied, and figuring he had covered all the basics, he headed back to the bedroom, removed his tee, and climbed back in bed. He slid the pillow out from under her and chuckled when she curled right back up against him. Jude dozed for about another hour before he finally felt her stirring.

"Hey my little rainbow," he greeted, when she lifted her head and looked at him.

"Hey back," she returned, as he watched her blink the sleep from her eyes. "You need to find somewhere else to stay tonight."

Jude rolled his eyes, annoyed that she was back to that already. "Get up, do what you need to," he told her, completely ignoring her comment. "I'll see what I can do about breakfast."

Then he slid out of bed and grabbed his tee. When he turned to face her again, he noticed she was staring at his chest, so he decided to use it to his advantage.

"I'm spending the night again tonight," Jude told her. Then he casually raised his arms over his head and stretched. He had to bite his lip to hold in his laugh as her eyes zeroed right in on his abs.

"Sure," she replied, and he knew she had no idea what he was even saying.

"Maybe I should just move in," he pushed as he twisted slightly, causing his abs to tighten again.

"Sounds good," she said, not taking her eyes of his chest.

"Perfect, maybe you can help me pack," he added.

She shook her head. "Wait, what?" she asked.

"You can help me pack," Jude repeated. "I don't have that much crap to box up. I can be moved in within the hour."

"Moved in where?" his girl asked in confusion.

"Here, you just agreed with me when I told you I was moving in," he chuckled.

She immediately scowled at him. "You ass," she complained. "You knew I wasn't paying attention."

"And why was that?" Jude innocently questioned.

His little rainbow turned a bright shade of red, then picked up a brush off the night stand and threw it at his head. He ducked just in time, and it sailed out the door and hit the wall in the hallway.

"You need to leave," she growled angrily.

"Can't," he replied as he left the room. "I need to make my little rainbow some breakfast."

As Jude headed to the kitchen, he could hear her angrily mumbling to herself. He caught the odd swear word and chuckled. Today was going to be fun.

Chapter 30
November

November jumped out of bed, still cursing at Jude. The handsome ass had spent the night, regardless of her protests. She loved sleeping with his massive arms wrapped around her though. For the first time in a long time she felt safe. Unfortunately, she had felt safe with her brother and his friends too, and she had to remember how that turned out. She didn't want to say goodbye, but she had to if she wanted him to stay safe.

November washed up, cringing at the sight that greeted her in the mirror, no wonder he kept calling her rainbow bright. A minute later she was dressed and hopping down the hall. She peeked in the kitchen, happy to see his head was stuck in her fridge.

November hopped back down the hall and opened the hall closet. She stood in complete shock, not believing what she was seeing. The suitcases she had placed in there were nowhere to be seen. She fumed as she shut the door and paced for a minute, while trying to think. Colin had moved once, and instead of using suitcases, he had packed his things in garbage bags. Determined, she moved into the laundry room, then stopped dead again when she noticed the empty spot where the garbage bags had been stored.

That man was a dead man November thought, as she hopped back down the hall and into her room. She quickly emptied the essentials out of her dresser and threw them all on the bed. After staring at them a minute, and having no idea what to put them in, she got an idea. She pulled up the corners of her top sheet, then untucked the bottom two and tied them all together. Smirking, she looked at her makeshift carryall, and decided it looked pretty good.

November left it there for a minute and hopped into the kitchen next. As casually as she could, she slid onto a stool at the counter and reached for her phone. She frowned as she saw it was dead and realized she had forgotten to charge it the night before.

"Are you done hopping all over the fucking place?" Jude asked as he turned and glared at her. The ass had found eggs and was mixing them in a bowl.

"If you don't like my hopping you can leave you know," she told him as she scanned the counter, trying to figure out where her charger had gone. When she couldn't find it, she glared at him. "Can I borrow your phone?" she growled in frustration.

"My cell's dead, and I don't have a house phone," Jude replied with a proud smile. November tilted her head and studied him. Lucy looked pretty pleased with himself.

"You wouldn't know where my car keys are?" she asked, knowing before she even looked, that they would be missing too. He shook his head no as he continued to stir the eggs.

"Okay," November responded as she jumped off the stool. "I don't really need them anyway," she told him, as she hopped back down the hall. There was silence for a minute, then she heard the spoon drop and his feet pounding on the floor as he followed her.

"Stop fucking walking on that," Lucy roared as his footsteps got closer.

"I'm not fucking walking on it," November yelled back. Then she continued to hop into the bedroom, grab her makeshift bundle, and fling it over her shoulder. She hopped back out, knocking him into the wall as she passed.

"Hey," he growled as he stared after her. "What the fuck are you doing?"

November continued hopping right out the front door and down the steps. When she reached the clunker, she opened the back door and threw in her bundle of clothes. Then she shut it and opened the front door. When she was seated she leaned down and searched for the wires underneath.

"You won't leave, so I will," she replied, as she found the wires she was looking for.

"Who the fuck taught you to hot wire a car?" Jude roared from beside her.

"My brother," November answered, as the wires caught and the clunker started. She slammed the door, causing him to jump out of the way, and threw the heap in reverse. Colin had given her the clunker for that exact reason. If she couldn't get to her keys, she could hot wire the damn thing and get to safety.

It backfired as she tore out of the driveway, causing Jude to dive for cover. All November could do now was pray he'd forgive her as she roared noisily down the road.

Chapter 31
Jude

Jude may have pushed his little rainbow too far. He knew she had problems with him staying with her, but he had no idea why. He also knew she was attracted to him. But whatever trouble she was in, was causing her to do stupid shit. She had run, when all she had to do was open up and let him help.

He pulled out his cell and hit Navaho's number. The biker answered on the second ring.

"She's gone," Jude growled when the call connected.

"No, she's not," Navaho denied, causing Jude to rub his temple in frustration.

"I just watched her fucking pull out of her driveway. I hid her keys, but the nut hot-wired the car and threw her clothes in the back. She took off a second ago," he complained.

Navaho chuckled. "Sniper told us her real name is November. That's a real pretty name." Jude felt like he was talking to the wall and lost it.

"She fucking left," he roared. But Navaho continued as if he hadn't spoken.

"Sniper also told us that him and Raid siphoned the gas out of her car before they left."

Jude stood there speechless for a minute. "She's not gone," he replied somewhat dumbstruck.

Navaho chuckled again. "She's probably a couple blocks away. You could most likely run and catch up with her. Raid, Sniper and Steele are headed to your place anyway, they should be there in a second."

"Thank you," Jude sighed as he relaxed slightly. Then he hung up on the biker, pocketed his cell, and took off down the street. He ran flat out, not even stopping when he heard the roar of motorcycle pipes directly behind him.

Sniper was laughing as he pulled up beside him. "There a reason you're running down the street in your pyjama pants," he yelled.

Jude gave him the finger and kept on running.

"I'm not into the butch thing, but you may want to hop on the back of my Harley," Sniper suggested.

Jude finally slowed down. He waited until Sniper stopped, then climbed on the back.

"Don't fucking touch me," Sniper yelled. "You sit as far back as you can. This gets back to Dagger we're going to hear about it for years." Steele and Raid snorted from their position on their own bikes as they all took off again.

Two and a half blocks later, they saw November's shit box stalled in the middle of the road. She was standing beside it, cursing and kicking at one of the tires. She looked up when she heard the motorcycles and gave them a death stare.

Sniper and the other two bikers stopped about half a block away. Jude climbed off and turned to him.

"You couldn't pull up a bit closer," Jude complained. But Sniper just laughed and pointed at November.

As soon as he turned, a shoe came sailing at his head. He managed to duck just in time.

"Who the hell taught you to throw like that?" Jude yelled at her. Then he thought about that for a minute and answered for her. "Never mind, your brother taught you," he sarcastically bit out.

He backed up as November started to head towards him. She had her sheet thing thrown over her shoulder, and her other shoe in her hand. She was now hopping towards him barefoot and obviously furious, and he knew she was ready for war.

Raid chuckled. "I think you should climb back on Sniper's Harley and make a run for it. Even hopping that girl can do damage."

Jude was about to tell the biker where he could put that suggestion, when suddenly there was a loud explosion. Jude watched in horror, as November's clunker exploded and sent her flying to the pavement. His girl was screaming as fiery debris rained down on her and all around her.

Jude tore off down the street, and he could hear the biker's boots hitting the concrete as they pounded after him. His heart was beating too fast, and he was terrified he would lose her before he even had her. She suddenly went quiet and stopped moving. Jude ran faster, ignoring the burn in his chest.

When he reached her, he collapsed onto the pavement near her head. Steele reached them first, and kicked a hot piece of metal off her leg, and another off her wrist. Jude then very carefully flipped her over, cringing at the large gash on her cheek. She was barely conscious.

"I told you to stay away," his girl whispered. "I don't want you hurt," she got out faintly before she passed out.

Chapter 32
Jude

Jude had no idea what to do. He knew he was panicking, and he couldn't think straight at all. He had his girl in his arms, and the state she was in terrified him. Suddenly Raid and Sniper made it to them.

"Flip her back over," Sniper ordered, as he dropped down beside him. "I saw Steele kick off the burning metal. I need to see the wound."

Jude didn't even think, he just held her head and rolled her back to her stomach.

"Raid, there's a gas station on the corner, fucking move," Sniper ordered. Then he pulled out a knife and starting hacking at November's jeans. "The denim's still hot," he explained, as he was cutting. "I need to get it away from the injury."

Jude could only watch as Sniper sliced them up the side and then hacked them off. Jude stared at the ugly red burn in concern. He heard Steele on his phone, but he no idea who the biker was talking to. He could also hear sirens, and he hoped that meant Darren had arrived, and not some fucking beat cop.

Jude looked up just as Raid came back with his arms full of bottles of water. He dropped them on the ground then knelt beside Sniper, opening a bottle quickly and passing it to him. Jude stared in concern, as Sniper poured the water on her burned skin. November bucked and whimpered, then woke and screamed.

Instantly Steele dropped down and held her still. Raid continued to open the bottles and pass them to Sniper, who kept pouring them on her leg.

"You're hurting her," Jude roared, as he tried to stop Raid from opening more.

"No we're not," Raid growled as he pushed Jude back. "We were in the marines, we know how to treat a shrapnel burn. The first thing we need to do is stop it from burning. The water will do that," he insisted.

"I'm moving to her wrist," Sniper yelled. Then Raid opened the rest of the bottles and passed them to Sniper. All Jude could do was brush the hair out of her eyes and hold her head, trusting the bikers to help her. He breathed a sigh of relief when she passed out again.

Darren arrived next. "I've got my car, you can use it to take her to hospital. The fire departments right behind me," he told them.

"Someone blew up her car," Raid grunted. "The last place she needs to be is the damn hospital."

Jude looked at him in horror. "You think someone put a bomb on her fucking car?" he roared.

"Makes sense," Sniper agreed. "I bet someone set it to go off five minutes after it was started. Most likely they hooked it up to a timer."

"So if you two hadn't siphoned the fucking gas," Jude replied, not wanting to finish that sentence. "Fuck me," he cried as the implications ran through his mind.

"You get her to the compound, and you soak those burns in cold water. No ice," Sniper ordered. "Then cover them in Saran Wrap and wait for Doc.

He wasn't there when we left, but I'm sure Steele's already called him. Raid will drive, he knows what he's doing, so fucking listen to him," Sniper ordered.

Darren threw Raid the keys, then turned to Sniper. "You staying?" he questioned.

"There's a fucking bomb in that debris. I'm finding it," Sniper growled.

Steele grabbed Jude's shoulder then, to get his attention. "Pick her up, and get her in Darren's rig. Raid will drive and I'll follow. Mario's meeting us there. He has information."

Jude nodded, then picked up his rainbow as carefully as he could, and carried her to Darren's car. Raid jumped in and powered it up. Then they were on their way. They were just hitting the main road when five Harley's surrounded the car. Jude nodded his thanks when he caught Navaho's eye. Navaho, Dragon, Trike, Shadow and Tripp had joined Steele, and were escorting them to the compound.

Jude breathed a sigh of relief, as his his heart finally started to slow down a bit. With the club for protection, he knew they'd make it there safely. And while he was soaking his girls burns, he'd be having a word with Mario. If Mario knew why this happened, then he would know too. And once he knew who the fucker was, he wouldn't be safe anywhere. It was time to stop being a nice guy, and let the outlaw side of him out. And he had an inkling he wouldn't have to do it alone.

Chapter 33
November

November woke, instantly realizing she was in a car. She was laying down, and Jude's scent was surrounding her. She reached up with her uninjured hand and gripped his shirt. She remembered being thrown into the air by a blast of some kind, but she didn't remember much after that.

"Hey my pretty little rainbow, hang on we're almost to the biker compound," Jude told her.

"No," she cried. "You'll put them all at risk. I can't go there."

"How about you let us worry about that?" Raid replied from the front seat.

"How bad am I?" November asked.

"Bad burn on the back of your leg and wrist. Nasty cut on your cheek. Could have been a lot worse," Raid declared, as he drove flat out down the street.

"You're speeding," she unnecessarily told him.

"Know that sweetheart," Raid smirked. "But your clunkers a ball of fire right now. I don't think my speedings a priority."

November sagged against Jude, trying to breathe in his strength. Then something else occurred to her.

"My phones in my back pocket," she said as she started to panic. "You have to get it for me."

"Calm down," Jude ordered. "You can call who you want once we get you safe."

"No," November argued as she attempted to sit up. She let go of Jude's shirt and tried to reach between them for her phone.

"Will you fucking stop that," he growled. Then he knocked away her hand and grabbed the phone for her. "The god damned things dead," he told her.

Immediately Raid's hand shot out, passing a cell over the seat. She grabbed at it and dialled the number she had memorized. It was answered after four agonizing rings.

"Who the fucks this?" Colin growled into the phone. "This is a fucking secure number."

"Colin," November whispered, as the tears she'd been holding in fell. "My car just blew up."

There was a lot of swearing on the other end, and she could hear him moving around. After a door slammed shut he came back.

"Were you hurt?" Colin growled.

"I'm fine," she told him. Of course Jude would hear that, and disagree.

"You're not fucking fine," he roared, loud enough for Colin to hear.

"Will you shut up," November yelled at him, not wanting Colin to know she was injured.

"Pieces of a burning car hit you. Do not fucking say you're fine," he roared again.

"Stop yelling at me," she yelled back.

"November," Colin bellowed into the phone. "Where the fuck are you?"

"I'm headed to The Stone Knight's compound," she told him.

"Stay the fuck there, I'm grabbing the guys and I'm coming to get you," Colin demanded. Then the phone signalled he had hung up. She handed it back to Raid.

"Colin's coming to the compound to get me," she told him.

"He can come, but he's not taking you," Jude argued. "He'll have to go through me first."

"And a shit ton of bikers," Raid added from the front seat.

"But it's better for you if I go with him," November tried to explain.

"No, it's fucking not," Jude growled. "Tell me what kind of fucking trouble you're in?" he demanded.

"I can't," she whispered.

"Fine," Jude said, as the car pulled through the gates of the compound. "I'll fucking know in a minute anyway."

Then Raid was opening the door, and Steele and the bikers were leading them into a building. Her leg and wrist were burning once more, so she closed her eyes.

"Open your fucking eyes November," Jude ordered with a bite to his words. She did as asked and looked up at him.

"Hurts," November told him.

"I know, but I'm going fucking fix that," Jude promised. Then she was gently placed on a bed. As she watched, Jude pulled out a knife and cut the rest of her jeans off. Unfortunately she was in too much pain to protest.

"Her top too," Raid ordered from the bathroom, where she could hear water running.

Jude sat her up and pulled her tee over her head. Then he covered her front with a sheet. She leaned over further to make sure it covered her completely.

"Is that a god damned bullet wound?" Jude roared from his position behind her. She tried to pull away and hide it, but he held her too tight.

"It certainly is," came a reply from the direction of the door.

She looked up and saw a handsome man in a suit jacket standing there. He was holding a folder, and he was looking straight at Jude.

Chapter 34
Jude

It thrilled Jude to see Mario in the doorway. He looked down again at the scar on his pretty little rainbow's back, knowing it was from a bullet. Jude was desperately trying to calm his breathing, but it was proving difficult. He looked from his girl to Mario and then back to his girl again.

"You were clearly shot, and you almost blew up tonight," Jude growled. "I'd like to introduce you to a good friend of mine. His name is Mario."

"Cut the fucking chit chat, and get her the fuck in here," Raid yelled from the bathroom. "Her burns need more cold water, you can have your discussion while she soaks."

Jude looked down at November and made sure the sheet covered her completely, before he scooped her up and carried her to the tub.

"Lower her down. I made it shallow, so she doesn't get too cold. Just make sure her burns are submerged. You took off her tee, did you see any other burns?" Raid questioned.

"No," Jude replied as he lowered her. She cried out from the contact with the cold water, then sighed when the water covered her burns. "Better?" he asked, as he sat on the floor beside the tub.

November nodded, but didn't answer. A minute later she rested her head on the arm he had draped on the side of the tub. He turned to see Mario had followed them in as well. The tiny bathroom was getting fucking crowded.

"Anyone else joining us for this meeting?" Jude asked sarcastically. Then three heads appeared, peeking over Mario's shoulder. "Fuck me," Jude grumbled, as Dragon, Steele and Tripp waved at him. "Leave the door open, and drag the bed over so you can have a seat," he sighed.

"It might be easier to drag the tub out here," Preacher chuckled, as he too joined them.

"Great another comedian," Jude sneered. Then he rolled his eyes as they did actually drag the bed closer and sat down. Mario moved further in the bathroom and leaned against the counter beside Raid.

"Would you like to tell them anything before I discuss what I've found out?" Mario questioned November.

"Nope, go ahead," his poor girl answered tiredly.

Raid moved forward before Mario could continue. "I'd like to clean that nasty cut on your cheek while we talk," he told her. She nodded slightly in agreement, and Jude could tell she was half asleep.

"You fuckers keep your eyes off my girl," Jude ordered as he eyed them all.

"Hey, we all have girls of our own," Dragon countered. "Except for Raid. And he's the only one touching your girl," he snickered.

"Medical purposes only," Raid clarified. "I know she's yours."

"Can we start?" Mario pushed. Preacher waved him on, so he continued. "November Carlisle, and your brother's name is Thomas Carlisle."

Jude watched as his girl tilted her head so she could see Mario. She looked shocked, but she didn't confirm or deny what he said.

"Your brother was a cop. He got a lot of information while working undercover with a drug dealer named Blood. Blood found out your brother was a cop and went after him. Unfortunately you were with him at the time. You were shot in the back, and when you fell your brother covered your body with his. He was shot in the heart and killed. They need you alive to testify," Mario finished.

Jude looked down at his girl, to see she was barely holding on. Tears were streaming down her face and she was shaking badly. He'd had enough, he lifted her out of the water, placed her on his lap, and held her tight. She clung to him a minute in defeat, then looked at Mario.

"Blood's in custody, but his brother wants me dead," November told him. "I was told protective custody wasn't safe, so my brother's friends sent me here to hide."

"And then that fucker Colin visited and led Blood's brother right to you," Jude growled furiously.

"Well you've got an entire club protecting you now," Preacher grunted.

"And you have me, Trent, and my men," Mario said.

"And Darren will be adding his name to that list too," Tripp added.

"That's a god damned army," Jude told her as he wiped at her tears. "You got nothing to worry about now rainbow," he promised.

Chapter 35
November

November shivered as she sat on Jude's lap. She was only in her underwear and covered with a thin sheet. Raid had stopped cleaning her cheek as soon as Jude had lifted her out of the tub. She was tired, sore, and her thoughts were a mess. All these men were willing to put their lives on the line for her, and they didn't even know her. That meant a lot to her.

"I need to get plastic wrap on those burns right away," Raid explained. "Doc should be here any minute."

"I don't want to move," November whispered. "I want to stay sitting with Jude."

Raid smiled at her. "That's fine." Then he wrapped her wrist and leg in the Saran.

When he was done, Steele handed Jude a quilt. All the men turned as she was stripped of the wet sheet and wrapped in the warm quilt.

"When's the trial?" Preacher questioned.

"Three weeks," November quietly told him.

"So we keep you on lock down until that time, then the whole fucking club escorts you to the trial," Preacher announced.

November looked up at him and whispered the only words she could. "Thank you."

Preacher nodded. "Stupid fucker should be a part of this club," he declared, as his eyes moved to Jude. "He thinks because he did time he'll ruin the club's reputation. If you got your fucking head out of your ass, you'd realize we don't give a shit about that. You're a man that has a lot of strength, compassion and loyalty, those are traits we admire," Preacher announced.

"Did you realize that you've been prospecting for a year now?" Steele chuckled.

"I haven't," Jude denied with a frown. November turned back to see Steele grinning.

"You work the shop, you run any errand we ask, and you come when we call," Steele pushed. "That's a fucking prospect."

"What?" Jude questioned in shock.

"You've been prospecting for a god damned year," Dagger confirmed as he walked in the room. "Do we need to repeat everything? Jesus you're slow," he huffed.

"I'm not fucking slow," Jude growled.

"Well then your heads fucked up. Do you not realize that we only let members of the club stay in the compound?" Dagger continued.

"But Mario stayed?" Jude replied, still looking lost.

"Yeah, but he's an honorary member. In his line of work he can't wear the vest. Apparently it hurts his street cred," Dagger smirked.

"Fuck off Dagger," Mario sneered.

As November watched, Preacher stepped forward, taking something out of Dagger's hand.

"Can you stand for a minute?" Preacher asked.

Jude looked down at her. "I don't want to put her down," he admitted. November shimmied off his lap carefully. She knew what was coming, and she wanted Jude to have his moment.

"I'm okay," she whispered. "Please just stand for a minute." She gave Jude a small smile of encouragement. He nodded, kissed her forehead, and finally stood.

Preacher approached and held out a leather vest. "We would be honoured if you'd accept this vest, and become a part of The Stone Knight's. You're a man that we'd be proud to call a brother."

November watched with tears rolling down her face, as Jude took the vest and shrugged into it. Then a loud roar went up through the room, and November realized most of the club was now squeezed in the bedroom. She blinked as she took them all in.

"We were gonna put Lucy on your patch, but Preacher wouldn't let us. He said it was a shit name for a biker," Dagger enlightened him.

"It fucking is," Preacher grumbled. "You get to stick with Jude. Unlike most of us, we don't really call you anything but that. We did the same thing with Tripp, so you're not the only one."

Jude smiled. "Works for me." Then he turned to look down at her. "How do you feel about your man being a biker?" he asked.

She smiled up at him. "Now my man isn't just a badass, he's a badass with a kickass vest," she said. Then she watched as Jude threw back his head and laughed.

"You're both family now. Welcome to The Stone Knight's," Preached roared.

Chapter 36
Jude

Jude had no idea how to feel. He was a part of The Stone Knight's now, and that was something he never thought was possible for him. But, November's shit just got real, and it was even worse than he thought it would be. Watching her almost blow up had been terrifying. If Sniper and Raid hadn't emptied her tank, she would have died tonight. And to see the obvious scar from the gunshot she had received, had devastated him.

Jude was dealing with more than just an ex that wanted her back, which was what he had assumed she was running from. Colin was an ass, but the man clearly cared for her, and had done what he could to protect her. Although visiting her had been a huge mistake. He was a cop, he should have known better.

Doc finally arrived, and he was thankfully tending to her burns now. He had given her pain medicine and had said the two marines had done exactly what they should have. If they hadn't acted so quickly, the burns would have been a lot worse. Doc applied a cream, then wrapped both burns. They would need to be checked twice a day and kept extremely clean. Luckily, she burned the same ankle she had sprained, so she would be good to go with a pair of crutches. If it was the opposite leg, she would have been in a wheelchair for a couple days.

Unfortunately, the cut to her cheek was deep, and she needed six stitches. Jude absolutely hated that. Even with a numbing agent, she whimpered with each stitch. He held her as tight as he could and wished he could have suffered the injuries instead of her.

The only good thing that had come out of this, was that she seemed to be accepting his help now. Before she had been running, and she had given him no personal information at all. Now, she seemed to be open about everything, and she was staying close to his side. It meant the world to him she was finally trusting him.

Doc finished the stitches and headed to his room. He left Jude with instructions to get him if his pretty little rainbow had any pain or discomfort. After Doc was gone, Jude took off his tee and placed it carefully over her head. He couldn't help smirking, when she sniffed the tee and smiled. It seemed to relax her even more.

Navaho and one of the prospects Snake, had gone to her house and retrieved his bag, so he pulled on his sleep pants and climbed into bed with her. As gently as he could, he maneuvered her to her good side, then draped her burned leg over his own and placed her burned wrist on his chest. Luckily, it worked out so the good side of her cheek was against his shoulder.

As soon as she was where he wanted her, Jude looked down to find she was fast asleep. He kissed her forehead and stared at her for at least an hour before he finally fell into an exhausted asleep himself.

Loud shouting awakened Jude the next morning. He climbed from the bed, popped his head out of the room, and caught Tripp as he hurried down the hall.

"What's the commotion about?" Jude questioned.

"Unknown biker approaching, and apparently he's some scary looking mother fucker," Tripp informed him. Then before Jude could ask more the brother was gone. He turned back to November to find her sitting up in bed.

"I want to go see," his girl insisted. Jude sighed as he took her in.

"But what if he's here to kill you?" Jude had to ask.

"Please," she begged. "I need to see him."

Jude nodded, knowing she'd fight tooth and nail if he didn't agree. He helped her get a pair of shorts on, then quickly dressed himself. When she went to grab the crutches, he ignored them and scooped her up. She didn't complain, which he was grateful for, and snuggled in as he headed through the building and outside.

The brothers were lined up near the gate, and they were all armed. Navaho and Shadow positioned themselves in front of him when he was close, and he nodded in thanks. November was straining in his arms though, desperate to see the gate.

After about five minutes they heard the roar of a Harley. The entire club was armed and ready as they waited for the unknown biker to appear.

Chapter 37
November

November could only stare at the gate, as the rumble of the motorcycle got closer and closer. She was holding her breath and refused to let it out until she saw who it was. Blood was a hardcore drug dealer, and his brother was high half the time. There was no way the guy could ride a motorcycle, so she pretty much ruled him out.

"Breath little rainbow," Jude ordered. She continued to stare at the gate, took one quick breath, and then held it again.

"He's here," Dagger bellowed, from his position at the controls. Immediately Preacher moved forward, flanked by Steele and Dragon. All three men had their weapons out, and they made sure they were in plain sight.

As soon as the biker reached the gate, the rest of the club moved forward, and it completely blocked November's view of the man. She huffed angrily, as she wiggled in Jude's arms.

"Stop fucking squirming," Jude complained.

"I can't see," November whimpered, panicking a bit. Then she heard Preacher's voice.

"Wrench you ass, is that you?" the president yelled. Unfortunately, with the roar of the Harley she couldn't hear the answer.

"Open the gates?" Preacher ordered. "And you better not fucking be here to cause trouble."

November continued to hold her breath as the gates opened and the biker drove through. She still couldn't see, and it was killing her. The biker stopped, and turned off the bike, and she heard his voice.

"Preacher, long time. Not here to cause trouble brother, just looking for someone. Heard your sheltering a girl, and I need to see her," the biker growled.

November finally let out a breath and gasped for air. "Put me down," she cried, as she tried to jump from Jude's arms. "Oh god," she said on a sob. "Please put me down."

At her words, the biker named Wrench turned his head in her direction. When they locked eyes, the sobs came out of her faster.

"Move," Wrench ordered the men in his way, as he stomped towards her. She watched him come as Jude thankfully dropped her to her feet, but he held her to his chest so she wouldn't fall.

The biker didn't say a word, he just snatched her out of Jude's arms and lifted her into his own. She clung to him, as his massive arms pulled her tight. She couldn't stop crying, as she hugged him back just as tightly.

"Fuck me," November heard Jude snarl from behind her. She pulled back slightly and glared back at him. Then turned back to the man who held her.

"You shouldn't be here," she said sadly, as she touched his beard covered cheek.

"It's the only place I should be," he growled back.

"Your beard's so long," November said as she stroked it. "And your hair." Then she started crying okay. "Are you okay?"

"I'm fine imp," he assured her. "Colin told me your car exploded. I came right away."

"Where is he?" she questioned as she looked towards the gate. Wrench chuckled and shook his head.

"He was on my tail for about five minutes before I lost him. Little shit never could drive," he snickered.

November grinned at him until he touched her cheek gently. "You got hurt," he growled. Then he held her with one arm, as he lifted her bandaged wrist and studied it. Finally, he turned to Preacher.

"How bad was she hurt?" Wrench growled.

"Five stitches to the cheek, burned leg and wrist. The ankle was twisted before the explosion," Preacher added.

"Figures," he smirked. "What did you trip over this time?"

"Nothing," November complained. And that's when Jude stepped close.

"She fell out of a god damned tree. Now hand her the fuck back," he snarled.

"Not until you tell me who the fuck you are?" Wrench ordered.

"I'm her fucking man," Jude growled.

"Well I'm her fucking brother," Wrench growled back.

"It's nice to finally meet you," Jude greeted. "Now hand her back."

Wrench threw back his head and laughed. "I like him," he told her.

"Well I'm holding out on my opinion of you until you give her back," Jude returned.

Wrench kept chuckling. "Fair enough," he acknowledged, as he passed her back to Jude.

"Fine, I fucking like you too," Jude finally agreed.

Chapter 38
Jude

Jude stared at November's brother Wrench. He was a massive beast, slightly bigger than himself, which was definitely a feat. He looked scruffy though, his beard looked unkept and his hair was unruly. Mario had told them someone had killed the man, but he had suspected that was a coverup.

"Let's move this party inside brothers," Preacher ordered. "We'll have this discussion in the common room."

Jude nodded his agreement and turned to head inside. Wrench was right behind him, and he smiled when November reached out her hand and her brother latched onto it. Trike held the door, and Jude passed through. He picked the table Sniper and

Raid were sitting at and sat down. Wrench chose the seat right beside him.

A minute later Mario and Darren walked in. Chairs slid across the floor as bikers and the extra guests got comfortable.

"Wrench and I go back," Preacher explained. "I got in a bar fight a while ago and I was alone. Wrench stepped in and saved my ass. The two of us took on a dozen. I'd trust the fucker with my life," he admitted. Wrench nodded his thanks, and Preacher nodded back.

"Explain how the hell you're alive, when the police reports say you died?" Mario questioned. Then he turned to glare at Darren. "Don't fucking ask how I got those," he said, as the detective opened and closed his mouth.

"So glad I'm out of that shit," Tripp chuckled. Darren just twisted and aimed his glared at him instead.

"I went undercover to get dirt on Blood and his organization. I got info on his clients and witnessed deals being made. I even saw him kill a fucker once, but that's when he suspected I was a cop. Some low life wanted to rise in the ranks. He followed me, saw me with my sister, then started following her. The ass caught her with Colin and the boys and put two and two together," Wrench explained.

"So you faked your death?" Tripp asked, but Wrench shook his head.

"Nope, didn't fucking have to," Wrench admitted. "Blood caught me out in the open one day. He shot imp in the back before I even knew what was happening. Got me too. I went down hard, but fell so I covered her. Colin and the boys were around the corner. They took Blood fucking down," Wrench told them. Then he took a minute before continuing.

"Bullet nicked my heart. Died twice in the fucking ambulance. Colin swore the staff to secrecy and told everyone I was dead. I've been in the hospital ever since. Fucker saw November get up, she was gutted when she got a look at me, thought I was dead. Couldn't say she died too when she was screaming like a banshee," Wrench said.

"Colin gave her a fake ID and got her the hell out of there. Blood's brother wants her dead, and if he finds out I'm alive, I'm dead too. Which if he's watching this place, he'll already know," Wrench finished.

"You never should have come," November huffed.

Wrench leaned over and kissed her head. "Not going to let him get you imp."

"So the trial's in two weeks?" Jude questioned, and Wrench nodded. "We need to keep you out of sight until then."

"I'm not one hundred percent yet either," Wrench said. "Bullet did a lot of fucking damage."

"What the fuck are you like at one hundred percent?" Dagger asked curiously.

"You ever see a wrecking ball," November grinned. "That's my brother."

"Jesus, remind me not to piss him off," Dagger snickered.

"So if you're such a badass, how the fuck is your sister such a klutz," Jude asked. Then he growled when November swatted him.

"Our mom met our dad when she ran him down with her bicycle. He was walking down the street, and she swears she didn't see him. He ended up with a bruise and she broke her arm," Wrench chuckled.

"Jesus, it runs in the family. When we have kids, we're going to have to invest in a shit ton of bubble wrap," Jude snorted.

Before he could utter another word November shifted so quickly, she knocked the chair over backwards. He had to roll and hold her, so she didn't hit the floor. When he looked up at her angrily, the klutz kissed him, and he didn't care how many sets of eyes were on them. He kissed her the fuck back.

Chapter 39
November

November squealed when she was lifted off Jude. Then she turned red when she glanced over her shoulder and saw it was her brother holding her.

"Could you not jump the man when I'm in the room?" Wrench growled.

"But he's hot," November told him.

Wrench rolled his eyes. "That's no excuse," he sighed in annoyance.

"He said he wants babies with me," November added.

"And that I definitely don't need to hear," her brother growled. Then he carefully sat her in his chair, and glared down at Jude, who was smirking from his position on the floor.

"What are you fucking smiling about?" Wrench sneered.

"She said I was hot," Jude grinned. "And I didn't even have my shirt off that time."

"Fuck me," Wrench huffed. "You two make quite a pair." Then he planted his boot on Jude's chest and turned serious. Jude stopped smirking and stared up at November's brother.

"You fucking claiming her?" Wrench growled.

"I fucking claimed her the minute she pulled up in that crap car," Jude growled back.

Then Jude laughed, as Wrench turned quickly and placed his hand on November's chest. "Do not fucking move," he ordered her. She could only stare down at Jude as tears pooled in her eyes.

"Jesus, she's going to cry again. Get your god damned boot off my chest so I can hold her while she does it," Jude demanded.

Wrench nodded, removed his boot, and held out his hand. Jude took it and let the biker pull him to his feet. Then November was back in his arms.

"God damn it," Dagger yelled a little too enthusiastically. "It's like a fucking soap opera. Brother got shot in the heart but didn't die. Sister was almost blown up in a car crash. Man declares his undying love for her. I need popcorn," he shouted at Navaho.

"Fuck you," Navaho shouted back.

Then Dagger's phone rang. He answered it, listened for a minute, then hung up.

"I put Snake on the gate," Dagger announced as he turned to address Preacher. "There's a car pulling up. It's full of men, but Snake has never met Colin, so he doesn't know if it's him driving."

"Timing's about right," Wrench said.

"Right," Preacher replied. "Let's check it out."

Jude lifted her up again and headed for the door.

"I need my crutches," she told him.

"You don't," Jude denied as he ignored her and kept walking.

"Your going to get sick of carting me around all the time," November tried to explain.

"Best feeling ever is when I have you in my arms," Jude grinned. Then he winced as a smack landed on the back of his head.

"Don't fucking make her cry again," Wrench ordered.

"But they're happy tears," November yelled at her brother. "Don't fucking hit him again."

"Don't say fucking," Wrench yelled back.

"This is better than when the detectives come around," Dagger laughed as he watched them arguing.

"Hey," Darren complained. "Leave me out of it."

Then the group stopped as they reached the gate. November could clearly see Colin sitting in the drivers seat.

"It's them, let them in," Wrench announced. Slowly the gates opened and Colin pulled through. Once he stepped out of the car though November gasped.

"What happened to you?" she cried, as she stared at his black eye.

"Your brother," Colin answered.

"You punched him?" she asked Wrench.

"He's the idiot that led the fucker here," Wrench accused, as he threw up his arms in obvious frustration. "He's damn lucky that's all I did."

"I did that," Colin admitted sadly. "I don't even know how to tell you how sorry I am," he replied as he face her.

"It's okay," November told Colin.

"It's fucking not," both Wrench and Jude said at once. She blinked as she looked at both of them.

"Great, now I have two Neanderthals to deal with," she complained. Then she squealed when Aaron and Brent got out of the car.

"Put me down," she ordered Jude happily.

But he ignored her, as he turned and headed back to the clubhouse.

"Lucy, I need to say hi," November yelled.

"Don't fucking call me Lucy," Jude yelled back. "And I saw the way Colin said hi, those two can find their own woman to say hi too."

"Lucy?" Wrench asked in confusion, as Jude was walking away.

"Short for Lucifer," November yelled at her brother. Then she squealed when Jude bit her ear and sent shivers throughout her body.

"We have to go now", she told everyone unnecessarily. "Lucy's in a mood." Then they entered the clubhouse, and she lost sight of them all.

Chapter 40
Jude

Jude carried his pretty little rainbow down the hall and headed back to his room. Doc had left medical supplies and had shown him how to treat and redress her wounds. He knew it was time to take care of that. Their main concern was an infection, and Jude didn't want her to suffer that.

He pushed open the door to the room they had assigned him and froze. The entire thing was frigging rainbows. There were giant rainbows painted on each wall, the bedding was a bright patchwork quilt, the pillows had rainbows on them, and there was a rainbow rug beside the bed. He'd need fucking sunglasses every time he entered the damned room. He was only gone a short time, he had no idea how this was pulled off.

Then his rainbow bounced in his arms excitedly. "Sniper and Raid told me about this. It means your family now, and you've been fully accepted."

"Fuck me," Jude growled. "I'm in for it now."

"We're in for it now," November corrected. "You said you want babies with me, no take backs."

Jude smirked down at her, loving this side of her. "A partner in crime," he declared. "But somehow I think you're only going to get me into more trouble."

"I will not," his girl frowned.

"Oh you will," Jude returned. "But our life together will be anything but boring."

"Can we start now," November whispered, as she looked up at him shyly.

Jude kicked the door shut, and he headed for the ridiculous bed. Once he had laid her down he followed, covering her with his body. Immediately, her tiny hands pushed his new vest aside, and went directly to his chest. He couldn't help chuckling.

"Why are you so fascinated with my chest?" he asked.

"It's so colourful," November grinned. "I love all the tattoos. And it's so hard I bet if I ran at it flat out, it would feel like running into a brick wall."

"You're a nut," Jude said, shaking his head.

"No I'm not," she corrected. "I'm a rainbow."

Jude threw back his head and laughed. "You are. And now we have a fucking room to match."

"Are you happy?" she suddenly questioned.

Jude stopped laughing and stared at her. "I am," he admitted. "I never thought I'd ever settle down. There's never been anyone I've ever been serious about. Then you came along. From the minute you pulled up I was taken with you. No matter how hard I fought my feelings, I couldn't resist you. I was always looking for excuses to see you. And you were so klutzy you were always providing me with reasons."

"Hey," November frowned.

"Hey back," he replied. "And I never thought I'd ever be a part of the club. I've done fucking time," he told her. "But I've always wanted to be a brother. I love the guys, and I love being a part of a family," he admitted. "It feels like I've got everything now."

"I love you Jude," his girl admitted.

"I love you too November. Let me make love to you?" he asked as he brushed the hair from her eyes. "Let me love you completely. I want you to be mine in every way."

"I want that too," she admitted. "I want to be yours."

Then she reached up with her uninjured hand and tagged him around the neck. Her eyes were misty, as she pulled him down for a kiss. He growled as he deepened it, causing her to sigh into his mouth. The next few minutes were a mad scramble, trying to undress her without causing any pain, and then strip his own clothes.

Again the girl just stared at his chest. "There's more to me than my chest," he smirked.

"Uh, huh," she replied without looking away from it.

Jude climbed on the bed and carefully covered her body with his own. Then with a slowness he didn't even know he was capable of, he sank into her warm heat. She felt like home, and he cherished the feeling. He made slow love to her repeatedly, being extra mindful of her injuries. He couldn't get enough of her. She was sweet, funny and fucking beautiful, everything he could ask for.

Exhausted, they both fell asleep, not caring at all it was still only early afternoon. Jude held her close the entire time, and slept with a smile on his face. Finally, his pretty little rainbow was completely his.

Chapter 41
November

It was almost time for dinner when Jude and
November woke. She laughed when she found
herself sprawled sideway across him. Her head was
at the edge of one side of the bed, and her feet were
at the other. Her stomach was draped across his
chest. It put her ass right up in the air.

"How the hell did you get yourself in that position?"
Jude chuckled. She immediately turned to glare at
him.

"Well, I didn't do it on purpose," she growled.

"I can't say it's a horrible view," Jude remarked, as
he grinned and patted her ass. When he raised his
hand, she hissed.

"You slap my ass, and that's the first and last time we'll ever be having sex," she threatened.

"I see the honeymoon's over," Jude pouted. "I've put out, now you don't want me anymore."

She snickered. "I think I'm stuck," she told him. "I feel like I've been run over by a truck, and everything aches."

He instantly lost his smile. "Shit", he said. "I'll sit up and carefully shift out from under you. Then I'll get you up and help you in the bathroom. Dinner should be ready, and Doc said we need to get food into you with the medicine. He warned me this would probably happen.

November held as still as possible as Jude sat, and carefully moved her so she was draped over his lap, instead of stomach. Then he rolled her over, and as gently as possible lifted her up. In seconds she was sitting on the bathroom counter facing him.

"I love you Jude," she whispered. His eyes softened, then he reached up and pushed her hair away from the stitches in her cheek.

"I love you too little rainbow," Jude returned. "But I never want to see you hurt again. You scared the ever loving fuck out of me."

"I scared me too," November admitted.

They spent the next ten minutes with Jude helping her freshen up and brushing her hair. Then the man left so she could do her business. When she was done, she hopped to the mirror, washed her hands carefully, and then stared at herself.

November didn't even recognize the girl staring back at her. Her cheek was a mess. The stitches were black, and even through the gauze Doc had placed overtop, you could still see them. And the whole area around it was one big bruise. Her eyes were glassy and had bags under them, and she looked pale. Next she studied her hair. It was long, which was how she liked it, but even brushed it was a wild mess. She never heard the door, as Jude opened it and came to stand silently behind her.

"What's the matter little rainbow?" he questioned. "The cuts will heal, the bruises will fade, and you'll be yourself again soon."

November nodded, as she reached up to touch a piece of hair. "Your right," she sighed.

As she watched Jude through the mirror, he narrowed his eyes and leaned in closer. Then he touched her hair the exact way she had and studied it.

"What colour is your hair normally?" Jude asked.

November widened her eyes in surprise, but then she shouldn't be shocked he figured it out. Jude was extremely observant.

"Light brown, with some dirty blond strands running through it," she admitted.

He immediately frowned. "Is it dyed permanently, or can we fix it?" he asked.

She immediately smiled. "It's a colour wash. The dye is in the shampoo. If I wash it with normal shampoo, it should come right out."

"Okay," Jude grinned. "Then let's wash your hair. I'll throw some towels on the floor and make you a comfy little cushion, then I can use the removable nozzle to wash your hair. You should be okay to lean over the tub for a few minutes."

No matter how much pain she was in, she was instantly excited. She nodded as a couple tears rolled down her face. How Jude knew exactly what she needed was unbelievable. The man was quickly becoming everything to her.

A few minutes later she was sitting on the floor, comfy in her towel chair and relaxing, as Jude worked his magic on her hair.

Chapter 42
Jude

Jude stared at November, as she watched him studying her. She looked uneasy, and scared about what his reaction would be. It had taken him twenty minutes, and he had washed her hair three times, before the last of the colour had ran down the drain. Then he had left her on the floor, as he sat behind her and brushed and dried it. Now it was done, and he was in awe.

"You were absolutely beautiful before, but I can't even begin to tell you how much more you are now," Jude honestly told her. "The colour is stunning, and the dirty blond you described looks like stands of gold. You take my breath away."

He watched as tears suddenly ran down November's face as she cried, and he frowned.

"Don't you dare get your stitches wet. I was careful when I washed your hair, and now you're going to make a mess," he growled. "Stop crying."

"Don't tell me to stop crying," she yelled. "If you don't want me to cry, don't say sweet things that make me cry."

"Well I love you, so get used to me saying sweet fucking things," he yelled back.

"Well then, get used to me crying a lot," his girl yelled.

"Jesus," came from the doorway. "All you two have done since I've got here is yell at each other."

Jude frowned, but November squealed when she saw her brother standing in the doorway. As he watched she tried to get up, then cried out when it was too painful. Jude took one step towards her, but Wrench beat him to it. He was across the bathroom in two strides and crouching down in front of her. Jude was thankful he was in a pair of sleep pants, and she was in his tee and a pair of boxers.

Jude smiled, when November leaned forward and face planted against her brother's chest. Wrench's massive arms immediately wrapped around her.

"Scared the fuck out of me when Colin said your car blew up," Wrench growled. "I wasn't staying in that fucking hospital a minute longer. We'll do this together now imp," he told her.

"Okay," November agreed, as she started crying again.

"Stop fucking crying," Jude immediately admonished.

Wrench pulled back and looked at him. "It's a bad thing to cry?" he asked curiously.

"It is when she gets the fucking stitches wet," Jude explained.

Wrench instantly lifted his arm and wiped them off with the sleeve of his shirt. "It's nice to see your hair this colour again," Wrench said, in an attempt to distract her. "I just about had a heart attack when I saw you at the gate. I thought it was permanent."

November smiled. "Colin told me to do it," she admitted.

"Of course he did," Wrench frowned. "But darkening it isn't much of a disguise."

November shrugged her shoulders, then winced at the movement. Jude knew it was time to step in and get her some relief.

"Okay, that's enough," he said. "You can have your reunion in the common room. My little rainbow needs food so she can take her pain meds."

"Rainbow," Wrench smirked as he looked at Jude. "I see you've seen her with her pastels."

"Hey," November interrupted. "Maybe he calls me rainbow because I'm such a bright light in his otherwise dark life."

Jude laughed when both him and Wrench snickered at once. Immediately November picked up the shampoo bottle and launched it at his head. He ducked in time to watch it bounce off the counter and head straight back at her. Just before it hit, Wrench reached out and snatched it from the air.

"You got good health insurance?" Wrench asked.

"I did, but I'm thinking of getting more," Jude replied seriously. "It's going to cost me double anyway once I put her on."

She glared up at him, but then Wrench chuckled. "Let's get you up imp," her brother said, as he easily lifted her to her feet. Then he held her until Jude moved over and scooped her up.

"Lead the way," he told Wrench, as his rainbow snuggled in. They followed him through the room, and Jude laughed when November leaned over and snatched a tee from the top of the dresser as she passed. When he looked down at her in question, she smiled up at him.

"I'll never be able to eat with your chest on display like that, too distracting," she admitted.

"Jesus," he heard Wrench complain, but he didn't care. He loved that November was so distracted by his good looks.

Chapter 43
November

It surprised November when Jude carried her into the common room and she saw how full it was. As soon as they entered all talking stopped, and all eyes turned towards them. Then a huge roar went up, as the bikers cheered for Jude. She looked up to see him beaming back at them all. Then she heard chairs scraping the floor, as they pushed them out of the way.

"Hand her over before they get too close and accidentally hurt her," Wrench ordered. "I've got your vest, get your tee on so you can put it on over top. It will look great with the pyjama pants," Wrench chuckled.

November kissed his cheek, then reached for her brother as he took her and stepped out of the way. Jude barely got dressed, before the men converged.

"Are you okay holding me?" November asked her brother in concern. He leaned down and grinned as he looked at her.

"You weigh about as much as a pillow," Wrench smirked. "I think I can manage."

She laughed, loving the fact he was there to tease her. Then she looked over at the crowd that had gathered around Jude.

"He's a good man," she told her brother.

Wrench smirked as he watched Jude. "I know," he agreed. "He looks at you like your everything. And he's extremely protective, even with me. Thank god I don't have to kill him," he sighed.

November frowned. "You wouldn't hurt him?" she asked nervously.

"I would have if he wasn't good to you," he admitted. "It's been you and me for a long time, I'm not just handing you over to anybody."

"So you'll be sticking around for a while?" Preacher questioned as he joined them.

"I'm staying wherever my sister is," Wrench declared.

"What about your job?" Preacher inquired.

"I'll see it through until the trial, but after that I'm finished. A fucking bullet nicked my heart, I'm done with that shit," Wrench huffed.

"You just got here, and you don't know a damn thing about this club or the brothers, but I'd be honoured if you'd consider patching in. We've had a few bad seeds lately, and now that they're gone, we're making up for it. Your sister is a part of it now, and we'd love to include you in that family," the prez pushed.

November immediately grabbed onto her brothers vest and got his attention.

"You have to stay," she pleaded. "I don't think I could take it if I didn't know where you were."

"Being undercover so long, motorcycles and bikers have grown on me. I love the lifestyle, and I love the brotherhood the men share. It will be an honour to take you up on that offer," Wrench grinned. "But give it a couple days. Let Jude enjoy his thunder for a while before you let everyone know. I don't want to take his thunder away from him."

"Done," Preacher immediately agreed. "The club will have your back anyway, but I'm only giving you two days. Then you'll be a fully patched in member, with none of that bullshit prospect stuff. You've been riding for quite a while now, and you've had my back. I don't need a year to know your one of us."

"Appreciated," Wrench said. "It will be nice to be a part of this."

"Fucking hell," Jude yelled from across the room, interrupting them. November turned to see him pushing the brothers out of his way and fuming. "She's fucking crying again. She can't get her stitches wet."

"Well, that didn't last long," Wrench mock complained.

"Why the hell are you crying now?" Jude demanded as Wrench passed her back to him.

"I'm just really happy," November told him. "Your where you belong and I'm with you, and my brothers okay. It's everything I could wish for."

"Well, be happy a different way," Jude ordered.

She grinned up at him. "Yes Lucy," she replied.

He was about to yell, when two men entered the room with Colin and headed straight for them.

"Stop right there," Jude ordered. She laughed when he continued after that. "You can say hi from where you are. You can even wave if you want."

"See," her brother chuckled. "He's just the kind of guy I'd pick out for you."

Jude gloated then. "See, he said I'm perfect," he smirked.

Chapter 44
November

November was going stir crazy, and it had only been a day. Her crutches were a pain in the ass and she absolutely hated them. She couldn't move around very fast, and with her burned wrist it made holding them painful. As she moved down the hall looking for either Jude or Wrench, she passed Snake.

She turned sideways so the huge biker could pass, and accidentally hit him in the shin with her crutch.

"Jesus," Snake complained as he grabbed his foot. "Those fucking rubber stoppers hurt."

November turned to apologize, and spun the crutches so they went with her, when another roar of pain came from behind her.

"God dammit," Raid cursed, as he too grabbed his ankle.

"I'm sorry," she cried immediately. "I'm no good on these things."

It was then Jude came down the hall looking for her. He took one look at the bikers holding their ankles and started laughing.

"It's not funny Lucy," she yelled as she glared at the handsome ass.

"It fucking is," Jude chuckled. "You took out Dragon and Sniper this morning, and Trike last night. I think we're going to have to wrap the ends of those crutches in towels, or they'll be nobody left. That's five bikers already with limps."

Raid growled something, but she didn't quite catch it, as he did indeed limp down the hall with Snake hobbling after him.

"Your walking like that just to make me feel guilty," she yelled at their retreating backs. Then lifted her crutch to hit Jude when he laughed again. That was when her brother showed up.

"You two can't be at it again," Wrench sighed as he stopped to watch them. "And did I just see Raid and Snake limping? What is that four now?" he asked.

"Five," Lucy helpfully supplied.

"Six," November corrected, as she raised her crutch once more and leaned towards Lucy. Wrench laughed and blocked Jude as he got close to her.

"Put the crutch down imp and let Jude help you. You've got to rest that ankle, and the burn needs to heel, your pulling at it by moving around," her brother told her.

"I'm bored," she complained. "I need clothes, and I'd kill for my pastels."

Wrench nodded. "I understand. Let me talk to a couple of the guys and see if they can make a run to your house."

November leaned against him and sighed. "Thank you."

Then she squealed as she was scooped up from behind. Jude powered down the hall and into the common room with her, while Wrench carried her crutches.

"It's safe to come out," Jude yelled when he hit it. "Rainbow's crutches have been confiscated."

Bikers suddenly appeared from every direction. "I need to go to November's and pick her up some clothes and supplies, anyone feel like joining me?" Jude asked.

A few of the bikers headed towards him, as he set her down on the couch.

"Your brother can keep you company," Jude told her. "I'll get what you need and come straight back."

"Okay," she agreed. "But be careful."

"I'll be fine," Jude assured her as he gave her a quick kiss. "If Blood's brother is out there, he's looking for the two of you, not the rest of us."

"I don't care," November said. "You keep your eyes open."

"I promise rainbow," he smirked. Then he turned and walked away, with five of the bikers following him.

"He'll be fine," Wrench assured her. "I have my phone with me. We can listen to some music and you can clean me up. I've been in the hospital for a month," he told her. "My hairs a little too long, and my beard needs to be either shaved off or trimmed up."

"Trimmed up," November immediately decided. "And I like your hair longer, so maybe just a trim for that too."

"Works for me," Wrench agreed. "Can I trust you with a pair of scissors and a razor?" he smirked.

She smacked him in the shoulder. "You almost died," she whined. "I promise not to even nick you."

"I'm sorry," Wrench said sadly, and she looked at him in confusion. "I left you alone when I should have been by your side."

November immediately leaned over and kissed his cheek. "And because of that we're both here today. Now give me my crutches back and let's see how many more I can take out on the way to my room."

Chapter 45
Jude

Jude pulled out of the compound with Navaho, Dragon, Steele and Dagger. Snake was following in a truck so they could load up the back. He couldn't help feeling a new sense of belonging settling around him. He had the club, and he had his rainbow. It was an instant family, and he was fucking thrilled.

When they got close to his street, they could see smoke billowing up into the air. Jude looked over to Navaho, and the brother looked back at him grimly. He knew without a doubt that the smoke was coming from November's house. He pushed his bike faster and got as close to the house as he could. It was difficult with all the firetrucks and police cars parked everywhere. Darren spotted him immediately and headed their way, getting right down to business.

"Looks like someone took out November's house with a bomb. Unfortunately, the bomb took out half of yours as well," the detective explained.

Jude instantly looked at Navaho, remembering the day November pulled up. Navaho had joked that his rainbow would most likely burn down her house and take out his too. Jude had no idea then, that the bikers prediction would come true.

"Sorry brother," Navaho apologized, and Jude knew he remembered the same conversation. He nodded at his best friend in acceptance.

"I tried to get a hold of you, but obviously you were on your bike. It happened about twenty minutes ago. I figure, since the car bomb didn't work, Blood's brother is stepping things up," Darren informed them.

"But why would he take out her house? He should know she's not here. I'd bet dollars the fucker followed her to the compound, or at the very least had someone else do it," Dragon questioned.

"I agree," Darren stated. "But this way she's got nothing to go back too. He's got her cornered at the compound."

"Fuck," Jude cursed. "And no one saw a thing?"

"It's the middle of the day. Kids are at school and parents are at work," Darren sighed.

Jude looked up. "The fucking cat lady isn't," he growled.

But Darren shut that down immediately. "We checked, she's visiting her sister for the week."

"We need to get back to the compound," Steele ordered. "If he bombed her car and house, the compounds next."

Darren nodded in agreement. "You take off, I'll call Preacher and let him know what's going on. You want me to head over in a few?" he questioned.

"Nah," Steele replied. "If he tries to blow up the compound, we're going to fucking blow him up. Best you not be around for that."

Jude started his bike again, and the brothers pushed their bikes to their limits, in order to make it back to the compound quickly. There were woman there, along with Dragon's daughter Catherine, and they hoped like hell they beat the fucker there.

Not ten minutes later they were pulling back through the gates, and Preacher was standing at the doors looking pissed.

"Park your bikes down the back, as far away from the gates as you can. We've got all the woman, along with Catherine, sent to Mario's house. We have Mario's men on them, but he's here," Preacher let them know.

Then the prez turned to Jude. "Your woman wouldn't go, and neither would Wrench."

"Fuck," Jude raged, as he cranked his Harley and headed down the back. Once the bikes were stashed a safe distance away, the men jogged back.

"Sniper and Raid are on the roof, and Shadow's across the street in the woods. Navaho arm yourself with everything you can fucking carry, and go find Shadow," Preacher ordered. Navaho nodded and took off. "I've got everyone here armed and ready. We need to catch the fucker before he takes everyone out."

"Right," Steele agreed. "But we don't know if he's alone, or if he's found friends."

"Exactly," Preacher responded. "Jude, I want you to drag your girl up to Mario's house if you have to.

The rest of you scatter. Arm yourselves and pick a place with decent cover. I want all eyes on the gates."

Jude turned to head inside, but he was too late. The gates blew, and all hell broke loose. Four men ran in carrying dynamite, and bullets flew, as the bikers fired on them. All Jude could do was duck and start firing too.

Chapter 46
November

November stared at her brother as he studied his reflection. She had trimmed his beard a bit and cut his hair. It still brushed his shoulders, but it suited him, so she wanted to stop there.

"You did good imp," Wrench told her. "I could get used to this look."

"Well, if you're sticking around I can keep it trimmed up for you," November teased, as she smiled at him.

"You got it," he immediately replied.

"Will you be happy here?" she asked in concern.

"I'll be happy here," Wench promised. "I'll be with you, I'll be away from my fucking job, and I'll be able to relax and get back to full strength."

November beamed down at him, happy with his answer, then leaned over to kiss his head. He had dragged a bar stool in, so she didn't have to stand on her hurt leg, and he had just knelt on the floor in front of her. She knew it was uncomfortable for him, but he wouldn't budge. She shrugged and had gotten work, because that's just how her brother was.

"You seem happy with Jude," Wench commented, and she couldn't help but smile.

"He kind of powered his way into my life. He's big, he's demanding, and he takes my breath away. We fight, but it's a good fighting," she admitted. "I love him."

"I'm happy for you imp," he told her.

Wench would have said more, but the sound of an explosion out front stopped them cold.

"What was that?" November asked quietly. Then she listened as feet pounded down the hall, and men started yelling.

"You have to go see what's going on?" she told her brother. But he only frowned down at her.

"I'm not fucking leaving you," he growled.

"You have to," she pleaded. "This whole club has put their lives on the line to help us. If it's Blood's brother, you need to help."

Wrench nodded in agreement, but still looked torn. "I need to make you safe first," he decided.

She knew he needed that, so she grabbed her crutches and motioned towards the door. He produced a gun from the waistband of his pants and quietly opened it. She hobbled on the crutches after him, as he made his way down the hall.

The first man they ran into was Preacher. He instantly turned furious their way. "Where the hell have you two been? Steele called ten minutes ago and warned us of an attack, but we couldn't find you two fuckers."

Wrench's eyes turned scary, and November knew he was pissed. "We were in the bathroom and November was cutting my hair. What the hell is going on?"

Preacher sighed. "Blood's brother blew up Novembers house, and we figure the compounds next. I sent Sniper and Raid to the roof, and I've got Shadow across the street. Every brother is prepared." Then he turned to her. "Girls have gone up to Mario's fortress on the hill. I want you with them."

"No," November immediately answered.

"Fuck me," Preacher growled, at the same time her brother yelled, "god dammit imp."

"I'm a part of this, and I'm not drawing anybody to where the girls are," she stubbornly told them.

"You think we can't handle this?" Preacher questioned furiously.

"I have no doubt you can," she immediately responded. "But I'm not willing to risk it."

"I don't have time for this," Preacher yelled, as he rubbed the back of his neck.

Just then Colin ran into the room. "Colin," she yelled. He skidded to a stop and ran their way.

"Stay with me so my brother can go help," she demanded. Then she turned back to her brother.

"I'll be fine with him, now go do what you need to do so this ends."

Wrench glared at Colin, and the man nodded his head. Then Wrench nodded back and turned to her.

"You stay fucking safe," Wrench ordered as he took off out the back door. Preached studied her a minute, then turned and headed out front.

"We need to get you somewhere safe," Colin declared as he scooped her up.

"You bring all your police officer stuff?" she asked.

"Police officer stuff?" Colin questioned in confusion.

"Yeah," November quickly confirmed. "All the stuff you carried in that bag."

"It's in the room they let me use," he answered, still looking unsure.

"Then that's the safest place," she noted.

November knew he agreed, when he turned and headed that way. She smiled as a plan began to form in her head.

Chapter 47
Jude

Jude hunkered down against the side of the building and pulled out his gun. There were five men running into the compound, and they all had sticks of dynamite in their hands. They were close to the gates, but within seconds they would be in a position where if they threw it, they could take out a building.

There was a commotion inside the main building, then Dagger ran out with a crazy look on his face. As Jude watched, he pulled a gun while still running and fired. There was a huge explosion, and Jude was stunned to see the man was no longer there.

"Shoot the fucking dynamite," Dagger bellowed in frustration, as he aimed at another man and fired.

Suddenly every biker there stood with their guns raised, picked a target, and fired. At once, all the men with the dynamite exploded. The sound was unbelievable, and their death was worse. Blood and body parts rained down everywhere. Luckily, the men were far enough back that nothing of importance was hit, and not one biker got hurt.

They only got a minute to regroup before another group of men ran into the compound. This time they were armed with guns. Once more, the bikers took cover and fired. Jude took out two himself before they entered the compound. When a shot fired from beside him, he turned to see Wrench crouched there.

"Where's November?" Jude yelled over the gunfire.

"She's inside with Colin," her brother yelled back. Jude nodded, satisfied that she was safe, and continued to fire. He was guarding the door, and he knew no one would get past either him or Wrench.

Jude was pleased to see that most of the men attacking them had been taken out, and the few that were left were being picked off by Sniper and Raid from the roof. The bikers were top shots with their rifles. Everyone they hit went down.

Suddenly, when things were quieting down, his attention was drawn to the back of the building. Jude's whole body locked solid as November came hobbling out. She was going as fast as she could, and she didn't have her crutches. Terrified, he got up and started moving before anybody else saw her.

"Hey," his girl screamed as loud as she could gaining everyone's attention. All the surrounding gunfire stopped as everyone turned her way. "You want me, come out and show yourself you coward. You killed my brother, and I'm going to testify and put your brother away for life."

Jude was still running, and he noticed Wrench was now up as well. The two of them were too far away though, and there were no bikers any closer.

"You fucking bitch," a wiry man yelled, as he ran flat out into the compound, eyes directly on her. "I'm going to fucking end you."

Jude watched in horror as the man was shot three times, but managed to get off two shots of own. He turned, completely devastated to see both shots hitting his rainbow directly in the chest. She flew backwards with the force and landed hard on the pavement.

Both him and Wrench opened fire on Blood's brother until they ran out of bullets. The rest of the bikers fired as well, taking out the rest of his men.

Finally all was quiet. But Jude didn't notice, he was screaming his girls name as he ran for her. He didn't even noticed that Wrench tore after him. He collapsed to his knees as soon as he reached her.

Jude stared down into her open eyes. "Rainbow," he cried as he lifted her head. He was horrified to see blood on his hand.

"Lucy," she whispered in return, then she turned to her brother and smiled.

Jude held her as Wrench furiously ripped at her shirt. He froze in shock when he saw the bulletproof vest she had on. There were two bullets embedded in front. When he heard pounding feet, he looked up to see bikers surrounding them.

"I hit my head," November told them. "I didn't plan on that."

"You hit your head?" Jude roared. "You fucking got shot. What the hell were you thinking?"

She glared at him, even though her eyes were hazy. "I drew him out so he wouldn't kill anyone."

"He fucking shot you," Jude yelled, not even trying to reign in his temper.

"Which is why I'm wearing a vest," his girl replied as she rolled her eyes. "I'm not an idiot. Now if you don't mind, I think I'd like to go asleep," she said.

Then they all watched as his rainbow passed out.

Chapter 48
Jude

Jude's heart just about dropped out of his chest when his rainbow passed out. She had foolishly risked her life, and when the bullets hit her chest, he thought for sure she was dead. He pushed the hair out of her face and turned to Wrench. Her brother was holding it together, but he was extremely pale.

"If he would have shot her in the head," Wrench said brokenly. "The damn fool took a chance she should never have. She risked her life for mine."

"November loves hard," was all Jude could say. "She protected all of us by drawing out Blood's brother."

"Crazy imp," Wrench huffed.

Then they both looked up and tried to see through the bikers, when the door to the clubhouse crashed open. Out came Colin, running flat out and in an obvious panic. When he saw them kneeling on the ground he sped up and dropped to the cement beside them.

"Fuck, is she dead?" he cried, as he stared down at November.

"No you ass," Wrench growled. "What the fuck happened to you protecting her?"

Jude nodded at Doc, as he pushed through the bikers and examined November's head.

"She locked me in the fucking bathroom," Colin yelled.

"You've known her since you were little. You knew she'd fucking try something," Wrench growled. Colin hung his head, and Jude could see the idiot was embarrassed.

"How'd she lock you in there?" Dagger asked, as he sauntered up to join them.

Colin looked up at him. "She shoved a chair under the handle."

"Amateur," Dagger snickered. "That should have taken you about a minute at the most."

Colin glared at him, then turned to Wrench. "How bad?" he asked.

Jude could tell Wrench was barely holding on. "She fucking ran out and started yelling. Got Blood's brother's attention. He fired two bullets into her chest."

Colin rocked back and fell on his ass. "Christ," he whispered. "That girl broke when you were in the hospital. She would have done anything to keep you safe."

"You think I don't know that?" Wrench replied, and the look on his face showed how wrecked he was. "It's why I had you watching her."

"That's enough," Preacher growled as he joined them. "Doc, get November in the clubhouse and see to her injuries. I want the rest of you combing the area outside the gates. I want to make sure all these fuckers are dead. Then we need to clean up. I know Darren will back us, but I want most of this to disappear before we're overrun by cops."

The men headed for the gates, and Jude had just lifted his rainbow to take her in, when Shadow prowled through the gates and whistled to get their attention. Jude stopped when he saw the brother was holding a rocket launcher.

"What the fuck?" Preacher cursed as he headed for Shadow. Navaho followed Shadow a minute later carrying his own rocket launcher.

"There's eight dead in the woods," Shadow smirked. "I'll need help to clean that up. There's also an arsenal out there. Besides these, there's two more and a shit ton of grenades. Blood's brother was taking this compound down, and he planned to flatten fucking everything."

Preacher turned slowly and looked at November as she lay unconscious in Jude's arms.

"So if she hadn't done what she did?" Preacher hissed, not finishing.

"Yep," Navaho confirmed. "We wouldn't be here right now."

Jude pulled his rainbow closer and shoved his face in her hair. The little klutz had saved them all.

"Get her fucking inside," Preacher yelled. "I want brothers in the woods and I want brothers here."

Jude turned to head inside, and he knew Wrench was on his heels again. That man was as protective as he was. Doc hurried ahead and opened the door when he got close. Jude strode down the hall to the clinic Doc had set up and placed her on the table. Then he stayed close as Doc got to work.

It turned out her head wasn't too bad. Doc was happy it was bleeding, he explained that it meant there wasn't any swelling. She would have a headache for several days, but three stitches and she'd be good to go. Her ankle was fucked up from her walking on it, but Doc said it only meant she'd be in crutches longer. Walking had also pulled at her burn, but again Doc assured him it would be okay.

Overall, everything was good, until Wrench and him got the vest off and they got a look at her chest.

Chapter 49
November

November slowly woke up. She was sore, and she didn't want to wake up. There was a pressure on her chest making it harder than normal to breathe. Something pinned her hand down, and she knew without looking Jude was holding it. She could feel the calluses on his palm. Her head was fuzzy, and she knew she'd been hurt again, but couldn't quite remember what had happened.

November carefully opened her eyes, then screamed when she found the handsome ass's face inches from hers. He reared back slightly in surprise.

"What the hell?" he growled as he held his chest. "You almost gave me a heart attack."

"I almost gave you a heart attack?" she replied in disbelief. "Why the hell were you in my face like that?"

Jude scowled at her. "Your hand tightened in mine, and I was hoping you were waking up."

"So you thought you'd put your face that close to mine?" she asked.

"I wanted to be the first thing you saw," Jude replied looking annoyed.

"Well you accomplished that," she complained. Then she looked around noticing no one else was in the room. "There's no one else in here it you?" she said in surprise.

"Right," he confirmed smugly.

November shook her head then and gave up. It would take decades to figure out how his brain worked.

"What happened to me?" she questioned.

Jude's smug look turned into a scowl. "You don't remember?"

November thought hard. "I remember a bang, then everyone was running and shouting," she told him.

"Uh huh," Jude grunted. "Anything else?" he angrily pushed.

November remembered being with Colin. "I locked Colin in the bathroom," she chuckled.

His anger seemed to ratchet up a notch then. "What about after that?" he said while gritting his teeth.

"Jesus Lucy, you look about to blow," she sighed. Then she remembered running out of the compound and yelling for Blood's brother.

"Uh oh," she whispered.

"Yeah, uh oh," he repeated. "That about sums it up."

"I guess something bad happened?" she whispered.

"You'd guess right," he snarled. "He shot you twice."

She squinted her eyes at him and tried to remember.

"What the hell are you doing with your eyes?" he said in exasperation.

"I'm trying to remember," November hissed, as she kept at it.

"And having your eyes look like that helps?" he complained.

"Yes," she replied. Then it finally came to her. She remembered him running into the compound with his guns out. And she remembered the pain in her chest when he fired.

"He shot me," November said in surprise.

"He shot you twice," Jude amended. "I thought you were fucking dead."

"Take your shirt off," she immediately ordered.

"Why?" he asked in curiosity.

"Because I don't want to remember that, and looking at your chest always makes me forget stuff," she declared as she sobbed. "I almost died," she gasped.

His face instantly lost its angry look, and he gently leaned down and wrapped his arms around her. She clung to him and let her tears fall.

"You're okay," he soothed. "I've got you rainbow."

November had no idea how long she cried for, before she got a hold of herself and pulled back.

"I can feel pressure on my chest, and it's harder to breathe, but there's not much pain," she told him.

His scowl immediately returned. "Because Doc pumped you full of pain meds. Your chest is completely purple from all the bruising. You also have about four stitches in the back of your head, and your ankles fucked from where you walked on it."

"Was anyone hurt?" November questioned.

"No," he growled. "You saved the god damned club. Shadow and Navaho found grenades and rocket launchers in the woods. If you hadn't run out when you did we'd all be dead."

She blinked as she looked up at him, then her eyes turned wide.

"I'm a superhero," she announced proudly.

"Jesus Christ," he huffed as he threw his arms up. "More like Super Grover."

Then he ducked as she picked up a bedpan and threw it at him.

Chapter 50
Jude

Jude woke the next night to find his rainbow sprawled sideways across his chest again. The only difference was this time she was on her back, and her poor body was bowed at a painful looking angle. He figured she probably did that because her chest hurt so bad she couldn't lay on it. He knew she was awake, when he heard her sigh.

"You laying like that so I can't stare at your ass?" he teased.

Jude chuckled when she snickered. "No Lucy. I fell asleep on my side, with you curled around my back," she informed him. "I have no idea how I ended up like this."

"I think you subconsciously love draping yourself all over me," he declared with a smirk. Then he chuckled when she glared at him.

"Maybe, when I'm awake and can actually enjoy it," she snorted. "Now, not so much. It hurts," she admitted.

"Well, I'm not surprised," Jude growled.

Then he carefully sat up and slid her down to his thighs. Seconds later, he had her sitting in front of him and he was massaging her back.

"Your hired," November mumbled on a moan, causing him to growl again.

"You moan like that and this will turn into something you can't handle right now," he told her.

November leaned back and gave him a seductive look, then whimpered at the movement.

Jude immediately glared at her again. "Knock it off rainbow. Until you feel better, sex is out."

She kept the sexy look, but added a small pout to it.

"Jesus Christ," he muttered. "That's not helping."

He stopped rubbing her back and climbed from the bed. Then she squealed when he picked her up and carted her to the bathroom.

"I'll help you get cleaned up, and if you promise to be good, we'll go to the common room for breakfast."

Jude chuckled when she got excited. That had been his fault though, for three days he had locked the two of them in his room. Doc was allowed in to check on her and change her bandages, and Navaho was allowed in because he could cook like a world class chef. He was also forced to let Wrench in, but the fucker threatened to break the door down if he didn't get to see his sister.

Brothers had pleaded, offered gifts, and even sent their woman, but Jude had ordered them all away. After what happened he needed his girl all to himself.

"I think it looks better," she said, as she lifted his borrowed tee. She tilted her head and studied her chest.

"Oh yeah," Jude said sarcastically. "The blacks a huge improvement over the purple."

She frowned and dropped the tee. "It looks awful," she whispered.

"It looks like you stopped two bullets with you fucking chest," he told her. Then he kissed her until she forgot about it.

"Why are you wearing a shirt?" she asked. "You never wear a shirt to bed."

He grinned and tagged it behind his head so he could pull it off. She gasped when she got a look at his chest. He had two giant bruises right where hers were, and they were an ugly black colour, exactly like hers.

He watched, as tears streamed down her face. "What did you do?" she cried.

"We go through stuff together now," he declared as he pulled her close. "If you hurt, I hurt. You never have to hurt alone again."

"Jesus, I love you," she cried, as she buried her face in his neck.

"I love you too," he immediately told her.

It took her a while to calm down, before he was able to pick her up and carry her out for breakfast. As soon as they hit the common room, the whole place erupted in cheers.

"Put me down," his girl ordered when the bikers got quiet again. Then she turned to her brother, who had gotten close.

"If you weren't shot in the heart, I'd punch you right now," she growled.

"What the fuck did I do?" Wrench asked. Jude chuckled because she looked ready to blow.

"You punched my man," she yelled.

Jude watched as Wrench's head immediately turned to him. "You promised me if I did it you wouldn't tell her it was me."

"He didn't you idiot. But you just did," she growled.

"God dammit," Wrench sighed as he rubbed the back of his neck. "I should have fucking known. Now I'm going to have to have eyes in the back of my head."

When she laughed Jude grinned. His rainbow would be just fine.

Chapter 51
November

November sat at the table with Jude and her brother. She was still mad at both of them. It was so sweet of Jude to want to share her pain, and she loved him even more for it. But she was furious with her brother for punching the handsome ass not once, but twice. Wrench had one hell of a punch, and she knew Jude had to be hurting.

"Stop," Jude whispered in her ear. "I'm fine rainbow. You need to give your brother a break."

She looked at her brother and sighed. He did look miserable about it, but she knew it was only because she was having such a hard time with it.

"I love you," she told her brother as she took his hand. Then she watched as he turned to her and smiled.

"I love you too imp," he immediately replied.

"Everything's over now. You still plan on staying?" November asked.

"About that," Preacher interupted as he joined them. "It's been two days, and that's all I agreed to," he said as he glared at her brother.

Her brother nodded, and she got nervous. Her hand held his tighter as she looked up at Preacher.

"Steele," Preacher yelled across the room at his VP. "It's time."

November turned to look at Steele, and watched as he nodded and disappeared into the kitchen. A minute later he returned, carrying two boxes. When she looked around, she realized the room was now full, and all the bikers were quiet.

Preacher went to talk again, but the door slammed open, and another biker ran in huffing and puffing. He pulled a knapsack off his back and threw it on the floor. Then he bent over and tried to catch his breath.

"Did I make it?" The new biker asked worriedly.

"Did you run all the way here fucker?" Dragon questioned as he chuckled. November eyed the biker, but she knew she'd never seen him before.

"My bike broke down just outside the compound," the biker apologized. "You said I'd get in shit if I was late, so yeah, I ran the rest of the way."

"Jesus," Steele snickered. "One of the first prospects we've had that fucking listens." Then she saw Doc hurry across the room to the biker.

"How's the leg?" he asked. "Running on it won't help it at all."

"I'm better," the biker said. "Still aches a bit, but it's better."

Then she watched as Mario's woman hurried across the room and jumped at the biker. He grinned as he caught her and hugged her close. November hadn't even noticed the rest of the woman and Mario were there as well. Then she realized Colin and his buddies were standing in the corner.

"Smoke," Mario yelled. "That's enough." The biker instantly lost his colouring and stepped away from Alexandria.

"Who's that?" November questioned Jude.

"That's Smoke, he's a prospect. He and Alexandria were in a fire together," Jude explained.

"Okay," Preacher yelled. "Welcome back Smoke. I assume you're staying this time?"

She watched as the biker nodded and then laughed when she saw Alexandria surrounded by a glaring Mario.

"Time to do this then," Preacher said ominously. "November, stand up with Jude's help please."

November stood carefully and leaned against Jude.

"Honey," Preacher said. "You saved this god damned club, and you put your life above all of ours. You've earned this vest and the gratitude of the entire club."

Then with tears in her eyes, she watched Steele pull out a vest and hand it to Jude. Carefully, he helped her put it on. She looked down to see rainbow was stitched into the front.

"Yeah, we almost had klutz put on it, but Jude gave us shit," Dagger admitted. Then she grinned while still crying, as all the bikers cheered.

"Wrench," Preacher yelled next. And she watched in awe as her brother approached. "You've had my back, and your one hell of a biker. You wanted a place to belong, well you have one here."

Then Steele handed a second vest to Preacher, and the president handed it to her brother. Wrench was stitched into the front. It stunned her to see he didn't have a prospect patch on his.

"You are staying," she cried, as she hobbled over and hugged him.

"Stop fucking walking on that," Jude yelled, but she could barely hear him as Preacher yelled once again.

"Welcome to the Stone Knight's." With that said, everyone stood and cheered.

Chapter 52
Jude

After they handed the vests out, Jude cleared his throat to get everyone's attention. When the room quieted he stood, placing his rainbow carefully on the chair, and turned so he could face her brother.

"I know you don't know me that well, and we've only just met, but I'm hoping you'll look past all that. I fucking love your sister, and I'd be ecstatic if you'd allow me to ask for her hand in marriage," Jude announced.

Jude had no idea how Wrench would react, but he glared at him anyway and dared him to say no. He scowled, as Wrench glared back just as fiercely, then her brothers face relaxed and he grinned.

"If it makes her happy, it makes me happy," Wrench grinned as he pounded Jude on the back.

Jude had to brace himself from the force Wrench used, and he knew tomorrow he'd have bruises that matched the ones on his chest. He'd have to remember to stay on her brother's good side. When he turned back to November, she was crying again.

"Stop fucking crying, I'm trying to propose," he yelled.

"Your proposing, I'm crying, deal with it," November yelled back.

Jude threw his hands up in the air, then he sighed and got down on one knee in front of her.

"I fucking love you rainbow," he said. "From the minute you tripped on your front step, to the first time you called me Lucy, I fucking loved you. You've turned my whole life upside down, and I fucking love it."

Then Jude reached into his pocket and pulled out the ring he had made for her. It was a teardrop diamond, and it was surrounded with small colourful stones.

"It looks like a rainbow," November sobbed, as he slid it on her finger.

"Marry me rainbow," Jude ordered.

"Yes," she cried, then she threw herself at him and knocked him over. He held her tight, making sure she never hit the ground, then he kissed her. The kiss immediately turned heated.

"Hey," Wrench growled from above them, as he kicked Jude hard in the shin. Jude broke the kiss and glared up at her brother.

"You going to give me a bruise every time I kiss her?" he grumbled.

"Yep," Wrench chuckled. "I'm a big brother. I have to protect her virtue."

Jude did an ab curl to get into a sitting position, then scooped his rainbow up as he stood.

"I hope like fuck you meet a girl with five older brothers that are all as big as you," Jude snarled.

Wrench quickly lost his grin. "That's not funny," he complained.

"Boys," November laughed. "We have a wedding to plan."

"No we don't," Ali interrupted as she approached with the girls. "It's kind of turning into a tradition to get married out by the lake."

"Yeah," Dagger said in a sing song voice. "We hang twinkly lights, we go barefoot, and Raid plays the harp."

"I'll fucking break another one over your head you ass," Raid shouted from the back of the room. Jude smiled as all the brothers chuckled.

"It's Tuesday now, if you're in a hurry we could have it Saturday night," Tiffany declared.

"Tuesday huh," November replied as she smiled up at him. "I think Tuesday's a perfect day to get married. Wanna marry me tonight?" she asked.

"Fuck yes," Jude immediately answered. "Sounds fucking perfect."

Then Colin sauntered forward. "That's great, cause me and the boys are heading back Thursday."

"So soon?" Jude snickered. "It will be such a shame to see you go." Then he yelped as his rainbow swatted him on the chest, right where one of the bruises was.

"Oh don't worry," Colin smugly announced. "I won't be gone long."

Jude could only glare at the ass. "Come again?" he growled. Then he watched as Colin chuckled.

"I accepted a job as Darren's new partner. Apparently Tripp's hard to replace, so the spot has been open for a while. I start in two weeks," he explained.

"What the fuck did you do that for?" Jude yelled.

"I heard it was a lot of fun out here, and I'm looking for some action," Colin replied with a grin.

November squealed, in what Jude assumed was happiness, and went to launch herself at Colin. Luckily Jude was fast, and he tightened his hold before she could move.

"Hey," she yelled. "I want to congratulate him."

"Well there's no fraternizing with the enemy," Jude yelled back.

"How do you figure that?" she asked.

"Well everyone knows he's a cop, and everyone knows I'm an outlaw," Jude explained. "We're just meant to be on opposite sides," he smirked. Then he kissed her again before she could argue with him.

Epilogue

That night Jude was proud as fuck to watch his rainbow walk down the isle towards him. One of the girls had loaned her a colourful sundress, and Doc had changed her white bandages to beige ones that blended in with her skin better. She still had her crutches, but Wrench was at her side to help. Of course every couple steps he yelped, when she caught him with a crutch, and at one point he had to catch her as she went down. After that Jude had given up and marched down the isle to scoop her up.

"Hey," November yelled. "I wanted to walk down the isle to you."

"Well, that isn't working out too good," Jude yelled back.

"Maybe Wrench should carry me the rest of the way, and you should get back up front," she suggested.

"I've got you now rainbow, and I'm not fucking giving you up," he huffed.

Jude heard her sigh, and then she rested her head on his shoulder and gave in.

"Well hurry up then," she demanded. "I want to be your wife."

He grinned then and sprinted the rest of the way to where Preacher stood waiting.

"Jesus," Preacher said as he shook his head. "I'm definitely changing your vests to Lucifer and Klutz."

"Hey," they both grumbled at once.

Preacher threw up his hands as everyone chuckled, and then he started the ceremony. Ten minutes later they were happily married, and Jude was kissing the fuck out of her. When Wrench complained, he just scooped her up again and once more ran down the isle, while all the brothers laughed.

Jude headed straight for the cabin that the brothers had someone construct without him knowing. Apparently they'd learned as soon as a brother even mentioned a girl, it was best to start a cabin. Jude was fucking thrilled too, because he didn't have to lift a finger.

When they stepped inside, it was to a colourful interior. The walls were a soft cream colour, but all the accessories were bright. When he looked in the corner, it was to see a shit ton of art supplies sitting there. Apparently the girls had replaced all his rainbows pastels, canvases and easels.

Entering the bedroom, Jude wasn't surprised to see all the accessories from his room at the clubhouse.

"Awww," November sighed. "That's so sweet. They're so thoughtful."

"Yeah, that's not what I'd call it," Jude grumbled.

He then carefully made love to his wife, mindful of the still healing bruises and burns. He sighed when he sank into her, knowing she would be his forever. Jude knew he'd do everything in his power to make sure nothing bad ever happened to her again.

Two months later, the entire club escorted November and Wrench to Blood's trial. As soon as they arrived, Jude pulled out a camera and took about a dozen pictures of Wrench in his suit. He figured he'd need them one day, even though

Wrench was either scowling or sticking up his middle finger in every one.

The trial went fairly quickly, and Blood was convicted and sentenced to life in prison. The roar of the brothers when the verdict was read scared the shit out of most of the people present, but none of them cared. November was finally free, and she looked incredibly happy. She hurried over to her brother and started jumping up and down.

"Stop fucking jumping," Jude yelled at her.

"My ankles fine," she yelled back as she continued jumping.

"You literally got off your crutches a week ago, and that was only because you sprained it again the first time Doc cleared you," Jude growled.

"That wasn't my fault," she fumed. "I was baking and dropped the can of non stick spray. I didn't expect it to grease the floor."

Jude couldn't help but grin. The damn girl was still a klutz, and Jude hoped she never changed.

About the Author

MEGAN FALL is a mother of three who helps her husband run his construction business. She has been writing all her life, but with a push from her daughter, started publishing. It's the best thing she ever did. When she's not writing, you can find her at the beach. She loves searching for rocks, sea glass, driftwood and fossils. She believes in ghosts, collects ridiculous amounts of plants, and rides on the back of her hubby's motorcycle.

MEGAN FALL

Look for these other books.

STONE KNIGHTS MC SERIES
Finding Ali
Saving Cassie
Loving Misty
Rescuing Tiffany
Guarding Alexandria
Protecting Fable
Surviving November
Sheltering Macy
Defending Zoe

DEVILS SOLDIERS MC SERIES
Resisting Diesel
Surviving Hawk

THE ENFORCER SERIES
The Enforcer
The Enforcers Revenge

Sheltering Macy
The Stone Knight's Book 8

Chapter One
Preacher

Preacher walked into the common room and froze at the sight before him.

"Will you get your goddamned tongue out of my sister's mouth," he roared. "I'm in the fucking room."

Shadow smirked at him as he pulled away from Tiffany. "Well, you weren't in the room when I stuck it in her mouth," the biker replied cheekily.

"Fuck me," Preacher grumbled. "Another god damned comedian." Then he turned on his heel and stomped to his office.

He pushed open the door, then promptly slammed it shut after he was in. He sat in his chair and placed his elbows on the desk, then leaned over to place his head in his hands. His club used to be full of badass bikers, now it was full of pussy whipped men. He missed the old days, the days before pink rooms and women drama.

Preacher tried to contain them by placing the bikers and their women in cabins, but that meant the clubhouse was getting fucking emptier. He tried to recruit, but it was hard to find good men worthy of The Stone Knight's patch.

Preacher looked up when the door opened and Steele barged in. "Don't you fucking knock?" he growled.

Steele grinned. "Why the fuck would I knock? All you ever do these days is sit behind that fucking desk and pout."

Preacher picked up a stapler and threw it at the brother, but Steele ducked as he chuckled.

"What the fucks your problem now? I heard you yelling from down the hall," Steele questioned.

"Fucking Shadow was making out with my sister again," he sneered.

Steele laughed even harder than. "They love each other brother. That's bound to happen. You just wait until you find a woman, then maybe you won't be so crusty."

"I'm not fucking crusty," Preacher roared. He picked up a paperweight to throw at the brother next, but Steele ducked back out the door. Fucker moved quick too, he probably got that from hanging out with Trike. Now that little fucker could move.

Preacher stared at the closed door and leaned back in his chair. Fucking bikers were dropping like flies, even Mario had a girl of his own now. He needed to start a pool on who would be next and make some fucking dough.

Sighing, Preacher gave up on the paperwork he had planned to do and pushed out of his chair. When he walked back into the common room, he was happy to see Shadow and his sister were gone. He headed to the bar where Dragon and Navaho were sitting and joined them. Navaho instantly filled a glass with a shot of whiskey and passed it to him.

Drinking was what he needed to do now, he thought. Get rip-roaring drunk, then pass out in bed.

"You okay prez?" Dragon asked after a little while. Preacher was on his third shot and decided to be frank.

"I'm sick of the fucking girls roaming around all the time," he growled.

"Ah," Dragon grunted. "So you're jealous."

"I'm not fucking jealous," Preacher roared. He would have said more, but his cell chose that moment to go off. He pulled it from his back pocket and stared at Raid's name on the screen. They had placed the brother on the gate today, so that meant someone was here.

"What?" Preacher answered in agitation.

"Car pulled up to the gate. Man and woman inside. Apparently they're family of Snake's," Raid told him.

"Call the brother and have him meet me at the gate. I'm on my way," Preacher ordered.

"Right," Raid responded before hanging up.

He turned to Dragon. "Snake has family at the gate. Care to join me?" he asked his Sargent at Arms.

"Wouldn't miss it," Dragon agreed, as he pushed out of his chair and followed Preacher out the door.

Half way there they met Snake. "You got family?" Preacher asked the prospect.

"Pop and his daughter," Snake answered.

Preacher raised his eyebrows. "Not your sister?" he questioned.

"No," Snake growled angrily. "She's not my fucking sister."

Preacher shrugged as they reached the gate. He had no idea what to expect. With this club, everything was a crap shoot.